D0342313

Double-Dare
to Be Scared

Also by Robert D. San Souci

DARE TO BE SCARED:
THIRTEEN STORIES TO CHILL AND THRILL

Double-Dare to Be Scared

ANOTHER THIRTEEN CHILLING TALES

Robert D. San Souci

Illustrations by David Ouimet

Cricket Books
Chicago

Library of Congress Cataloging-in-Publication Data

San Souci, Robert D.
    Double-dare to be scared : another thirteen chilling tales /
Robert D. San Souci ; illustrated by David Ouimet.— 1st ed.
        v. cm.
    Sequel to: Dare to be scared.
    Contents: Campfire tale — Best friends — The quilt — Circus
dreams — Rosalie — Mountain childers — Class cootie — Half-past
midnight — Laughter — Click-clack — Daddy Boogey — Grey —
"Gulp!"
    ISBN 0-8126-2716-4 (alk. paper)
    1. Horror tales, American. 2. Children's stories, American. [1.
Horror stories. 2. Short stories.] I. Ouimet, David, ill. II. Title.
    PZ7.S1947Dou 2004
    [Fic]—dc22
                                                2003026610

Contents

Campfire Tale

A few days before starting fourth grade, Michael Johnstone went camping with his father, Dave, for the very first time. He had hoped it would be just he and his father making the two-day trek to Paiute Lake, but his father had invited a coworker, Larry Kinross, to come along. Michael didn't much like Larry. The man was loud and talked all the time and had a laugh that reminded Michael of the Martians' *ack-ackack* on his friend Zane's *Mars Attacks!* DVD. Worst of all, Larry always called him "Shorty," which he *hated.*

The first evening, they found a nice spot to pitch their tents on the way to the lake. Each had his own pup tent. Michael's had been purchased especially for the trip at the sporting goods store, where he'd also obtained boots, a fishing rod, and other gear. While he unrolled his sleeping bag, the men built a fire in the center of the clearing, then dragged a fallen log close to it to use as a bench. There was a little screen of brush between the smaller clearing with the tents and the bigger one with the fire.

By the time they finished dinner, the woods had become quite dark. It was a moonless night, so there was only a scattering of stars overhead to relieve the blackness. Michael nudged closer to his father on the log, suddenly aware of just how full of noises—chitterings and buzzings, cracklings and rustlings, hoots and yips—the forest was.

"Hey, Shorty," said Larry, who was seated on the other side of Michael's father, "how do you like the woods so far?"

"It's neat," said Michael, being careful not to let his uneasiness show, making him a target for Larry's teasing.

"Don't you wonder what might be creeping around out there? I always do."

"Larry, ease off," said Dave good-naturedly. "I don't want you scaring Mike."

The other man persisted. "I'm not scaring him. I'm just asking a question, for Pete's sake. Don't the woods creep you out, just a little?" He leaned around his friend to grin at Michael.

"They're fine," said Michael.

"No more," his father told Larry. "I mean it." He stood, set his tin coffee mug down, and said, "I'm going to use the little boys' room. You guys hold down the fort. And Larry, no scary stories."

"Scout's honor," his friend said, putting a hand on his

heart and raising his right arm in a Boy Scout salute. When Dave had gone to find the latrine they'd dug out behind the tents, Larry refilled his own coffee cup. Michael put another marshmallow on the sharpened end of a stick and held it toward the fire, watching the soft whiteness char to brown, then blacken.

Larry took a big *gulp* of coffee, then lowered his voice as though he were sharing a secret and said to Michael, "Your father didn't want me to tell you about The Stalker."

In spite of himself, Michael asked, "What's that?"

"No one knows for sure if it's some crazy person or some kind of monster like Big Foot or what. But he—or *it*—lives in these woods. He sneaks up behind hikers and campers and literally frightens them to death. Folks are found with their mouths frozen into an 'O' from pure terror. Usually he stays away when there are more than two people around. And he doesn't like a fire or any kind of light, so always keep your flashlight handy. If you hear someone creeping up behind you, turn around as fast as you can, yell, and shine your flashlight at him. But be sure to close your eyes. You don't want to see what he looks like. That's how he scares people to death. He's so horrible to look at that people just keel over from fright—or the lucky ones go crazy. There's a couple of guys in the loony bin right now who were found wandering along the shores of Paiute Lake a few years back. Their hair was pure white from shock, and their minds had gone completely. Hey, Shorty!" he yelled suddenly.

Startled, Michael nearly fell backward off the log.

"Get a grip, fella," laughed Larry, putting his hand on Michael's shoulder and pointing to where the boy's marshmallow had burned to a coal. The lower part of the toasting stick was burning. "You're not much of a cook, *ackackack*."

Michael pushed the ruined marshmallow and burning stick into the fire, while Larry kept laughing.

Dave returned at that moment. "What's the joke?" he asked.

"Shorty here is trying to burn down the woods," said Larry.

"I am not," said Michael, annoyed at just how much he sounded like a baby. "Larry was trying to scare me, telling me about The Stalker."

"Larry, I warned you." This time Dave didn't sound amused.

His friend gave a mocking soldier's salute. "Got it, General. No more bedtime stories for Shorty."

Dave turned to his son. "Those stories are just campfire tales people tell each other to scare themselves. They think it's part of the fun of camping out. I've never seen the point. And I think we can do without it on our trip," he added, looking meaningfully at Larry, who bowed his head and gave full attention to the last of the coffee in his cup. "Speaking of bedtime," he said to Michael, "I think it's time you turned in. Larry and I have a couple of things to plan out for tomorrow."

As Michael said good-night, his father unfolded a map of the area, and the two men began discussing the best route to Paiute Lake.

4

Michael lowered the flap of his tent and snuggled happily into his sleeping bag. Now he was even more aware of the sounds of the nighttime forest. But he could also hear the murmurs of the men and the crackling of the fire. He concentrated on these comforting sounds and soon was asleep.

But it wasn't long before he came awake and realized he had to go to the bathroom again. His father had warned him about drinking too much Coke, and Larry had kept predicting, "You'll be up all night getting rid of it."

He pulled on his jeans and shirt and sneakers and reached for his flashlight. Behind the thin screen of brush, he could see the fire, lower now, and still hear the men, who were disagreeing about some part of tomorrow's plan. Michael had been told not to go into the forest—even to the latrine—without alerting the others. But he didn't want to bother his father, and he sure didn't want to give Larry more ammunition for making fun of him, so he decided to make the short walk to the latrine on his own. He waited until he was around a tree before snapping on his flashlight.

He found the trench easily enough. Thoughts of The Stalker came to him even though his dad had assured him it was only a made-up story. He kept his flashlight on the whole time he was standing there. He'd just finished zipping himself up when something dropped onto his head. He grunted in surprise, and one hand flew up, launching the flashlight into the air to smack against something hard. He heard the glass lens break and saw the light wink out, but he

was too busy clawing at whatever was caught in his hair. He pulled something soft and furry and wiggly off and flung the thing away. "Ugh-ugh-*UGH!*" he muttered, disgusted.

Satisfied that he was spider—or whatever—free, he turned his attention to the flashlight. His dad was going to be mad if it was broken—especially because Michael had gone into the woods alone. Maybe, if he was lucky, he could find the flashlight, fix it, and get back to his tent before the men—still disagreeing over the best route—realized he'd gone.

He thought again of The Stalker, but avoiding his father's anger meant far more at this moment than Larry's stupid scary story.

He pushed deep into the brush and groped around, always on the alert for a spider's or other creature's sneak attack. He burrowed farther into the undergrowth. At last he found the flashlight lying against a stone. The lens was cracked but still in place. He tried pushing the on/off switch and shaking it several times, but it refused to relight. Well, maybe his dad could tinker it back to life in the morning. Michael planned to say simply that he'd dropped it.

In the dark, he suddenly realized he wasn't exactly sure how he'd made his way into the brush.

He took a step forward.

Something rustled on the other side of a bush. Something *big.*

He opened his mouth to shout for help, then stopped. Maybe whatever—or *whoever*—was there didn't know he was here. He froze in place, breathing as shallowly as he could.

The thing moved in the brush again. To his relief, it

seemed to be continuing along the way it had been going and would probably pass him by. He was sure he heard something like heavy breathing, almost *human* breathing.

The Stalker.

Don't let him—IT—find me, he prayed.

More sounds of movement, still heading away from him. Then sudden silence. A moment later, the brush crackled again. *Closer.*

It was coming toward him now. In a minute he'd be face to face with the horror.

Michael began to run in the opposite direction, slapping away the branches that grabbed at him. He ran until his side ached and he was out of breath. Though he wanted to gasp for air, he held his breath so that he could listen for sounds of pursuit.

But there were only the usual forest sounds around him. He had escaped.

Unless something was *stalking* him.

He scrunched himself into the fold of a tree trunk. He tried to stop shaking, but that was impossible. So he shivered and waited until his legs began to cramp. Then, when he was sure the woods were silent, he edged back the way he had come, trying to avoid making any sound that might give him away.

He realized quickly that he was lost. But just when he was about to panic, he spotted a faint glow through the trees. Relieved, he made his way toward what he now realized was the light from a campfire. He hoped it would turn out to be their own campsite. But even if it belonged to other people, he'd welcome any human company and the security of being where there was light.

Luck was with him. It *was* their fire. Somehow in his wandering, he had circled halfway around the camp. He was now coming out of the woods from the opposite direction. His father and Larry were sitting on a log in front of the fire. They had nodded off, their heads rested against each other, even as they slumped a bit forward.

Giddy with relief, Michael decided to play a trick on them.

Quietly, he crept up behind the two dozing figures. When he was an arm's length away, he suddenly reached out, grabbed their shoulders, and yelled, *"BOO!"*

Both men pitched backward off the log.

In the fading glow of the dying campfire, Michael could see the double 'O's of their fright-frozen mouths.

Then a twig snapped behind him.

Best Friends

At 3:30 in the afternoon, DeWayne Washington unlocked the front door and let himself into the lower flat, where he lived with his mother. Nikki Washington worked in downtown Oakland in a dentist's office. She wouldn't be home for at least another two hours.

Even though tomorrow, Friday, was the last day of school before Christmas break, DeWayne didn't feel particularly happy. The sky outside was gray and gloomy; the two-story house, on a dead-end street, seemed too quiet. His best friend, Rafael Vasquez, had gone with his parents and sister back to Mexico to be with relatives for the holidays. The Vasquez family lived in the flat above the Washingtons, and Raffa and DeWayne had been best friends since the Washingtons had moved in the year before.

Best Friends

The boys, both fourth-graders, attended different schools. Raffa went to the local elementary school; DeWayne went to St. Norbert's Catholic School, which meant a long bus ride to the other side of the city. But they had hit it off from the first, though DeWayne was small-boned and quick-witted, while Raffa was big and always seemed to think each word through before he spoke.

Most days DeWayne waited eagerly for the sound of Raffa's return from school, after his friend's football or soccer practice. DeWayne was too small to play—and his mother was afraid he'd be hurt.

It was never a problem knowing when Raffa was home. The other boy would slam the door and hurry upstairs, his feet thudding on the steps. When DeWayne's mom was around, she would often complain, "What is with that boy? Can't he close a door without slamming it or walk upstairs without sounding like a herd of elephants?" With a rare streak of meanness, she'd taken to calling him "Big Foot." Raffa's parents, both of whom also worked, were quiet folks who barely made a sound. To DeWayne, it was a mystery how they had produced a son who was so big and loud. But he was glad of Raffa's bulk and booming voice whenever they played together or went to a movie: no one would bother them the way DeWayne was sometimes teased when he was on his own, because he was so small for his age.

Raffa was the closest thing to a brother he had. He had been looking forward to spending a lot of time together over the holiday—until Raffa had told him, "We're going to Guadalajara for Christmas. My *abuela*—grandmother—lives there. I've got a bunch of *tíos y tías* who drive me crazy."

"You don't sound very happy," said DeWayne.

The other boy shrugged. "My grandmother yells all the time. My aunts and uncles talk only to each other or to my mom and pop. I have cousins, but the little ones are brats, and the bigger ones treat me like I'm *muy estúpido*. And my sister, Viveca, sides with them and laughs the loudest."

"Maybe you could stay with my mother and me," said DeWayne hopefully.

Raffa shook his head. "The family has to get together for our *vacaciones de pascuas—*"

When DeWayne shrugged to show he didn't understand, Raffa explained, "It just means 'Christmas holiday.'" So they had exchanged Christmas gifts the day before the Vasquez family took off. DeWayne had given Raffa a McDonald's gift certificate; Raffa had given him a paperback Harry Potter book, which DeWayne had already read—but it didn't matter. To him, sharing gifts was a reminder of just how close they were.

"Best friends forever," said DeWayne.

"Best friends forever," Raffa repeated. Then he put his arm around DeWayne's shoulders, gave him a hug, and went upstairs to finish packing.

The next morning, before the sun was up, a still half-asleep DeWayne heard the neighbors' van start up and roll down the driveway from the garage. DeWayne knew Mr. Vasquez was hoping to reach Guadalajara in five days, with brief stops in Fresno and Los Angeles to visit other friends and family.

*   *   *

Now, alone in the totally empty building, DeWayne went into the kitchen, pulled a Pop-Tart out of the cabinet, and poured himself a glass of milk. He got out the Harry Potter book Raffa had given him and decided he might be able to read it again. He let the pastry heat in the microwave as he began flipping through the first pages. Soon he was happily eating and reading, his loneliness momentarily forgotten.

Suddenly, he heard someone fumbling with a key at the front door lock of the upstairs flat. He wondered if a burglar was trying to rob the empty home. A chill went through him; he thought of calling his mom or dialing 911. Then the door opened and, a few seconds later, was slammed shut with all the force Raffa would give it. Next he heard footsteps trudging up the stairs—as heavy as his friend's but slow, tired-sounding, whereas Raffa always thundered up the steps. Who was it? DeWayne wondered. Anyone making so much noise couldn't be a thief. Could Raffa and his family have come back? Had they decided at the last minute against a visit to Mexico? Maybe someone had gotten sick?

He set the Harry Potter book on the kitchen counter. Carrying his milk and half-eaten Pop-Tart, he looked out the back window. There was no van in the driveway, no sign of anyone. From the living room, he saw that the Vasquez van wasn't parked in front of the house, either. But now he could hear heavy footsteps heading down the hall to the bedroom at the back of the flat, the one that belonged to Raffa. His room was right above DeWayne's.

Leaving his empty glass in the sink and licking a stray bit of strawberry filling off his fingertips, DeWayne walked back to his room. Now he could hear the feet overhead pacing in a circle. It had to be Raffa! Maybe his folks had dropped him off and gone to run an errand.

Then he heard knocking on the floor above—Raffa's signal to come on up. Well, he'd find out the answer soon enough. And the day, though still overcast and threatening rain, seemed less gloomy now that Raffa was back.

DeWayne let himself out his own front door and rang the bell beside the adjoining door. After a minute, he heard the slow, heavy footsteps coming down the steep wooden stairs leading to the hallway above. Again, he was bothered that Raffa was moving so slowly. Maybe he really was sick. Through the lace curtains on the glass-paneled door, DeWayne recognized his friend's hulking shape. Then Raffa yanked the door open, as he always did—as if not quite realizing his own strength.

"Hi," DeWayne said. "You didn't go to Mexico after all."

Raffa shrugged and stood back to let his friend into the little hall at the foot of the stairs. No lights were on, and the stairs were deeply shadowed so late on this gray afternoon. "You saving on electricity?" DeWayne teased.

Raffa shrugged again. Then, after a long time, he reached out and fumbled for the light switch, as if how to turn on the lights was something he'd forgotten for a minute.

"You okay?" asked DeWayne. In the light, Raffa's dark skin seemed almost pale. His forehead and cheeks were damp. DeWayne wondered whether he had a fever.

The other boy nodded. "Fine."

"Where are your folks?"

A funny look passed across the other boy's face. "Gone."

"When will they be back?"

A final shrug. Then Raffa started upstairs, signaling for DeWayne to follow. DeWayne did, puzzled by the way the other boy was walking—with the slow, painful steps of an old man. It was as though he were stopping and reminding himself how to climb each stair. Now DeWayne was sure his friend was sick with the flu or something. His parents must have gone for medicine—probably to the *farmacia* downtown where they always shopped. It was surprising that one of them, or Raffa's older sister, Viveca, hadn't stayed with the boy, but that was their business.

No lights were on upstairs, though skylights let in a watery grayness from outside. Uncomfortable with the gloom, DeWayne began snapping on lights. His friend, shuffling toward his own bedroom, didn't seem to notice or care.

When they reached his room, Raffa stopped in the middle and stared at his friend as though seeing him for the first time.

"What's up with you?" DeWayne asked. "You're giving me a funny look, and it's weirding me out. If you're sick, you should get in bed. Wait for your folks to bring medicine."

"No time," the other boy said sadly. "It's dark and cold and lonesome. I don't want to be alone."

"Then I'll wait until your folks get back. But you should lie down."

At this, Raffa smiled—a strange, crooked smile that made DeWayne even more uneasy.

Raffa's bedroom was off the kitchen. Some brightness

was coming through the doorway, because DeWayne had put on the lights there. But neither boy had turned on the bedroom light. Raffa was becoming just a shadow outlined by the fast-fading light from the room's corner windows—yet his skin seemed almost to glow. DeWayne reached for the light switch, but his friend grabbed his arm with unexpected speed.

"Don't," Raffa said. "I like the dark when it's not lonely."

"Fine, okay, but let loose of my wrist," said DeWayne. "You're hurting me." The circling fingers tightened. "Let loose!" DeWayne pleaded. "What are you trying to do?"

"Best friends," said the other. "Forever."

The smaller boy didn't say anything as he tried to twist free. But the other's grip held him as if he were handcuffed. "You're sick," DeWayne said. "You're not thinking right. *Let loose!*" All the time he was talking, he was straining to hear the sound of a van parking, the front door opening, footsteps of returning parents on the stairs.

Silence.

In the dark room, Raffa was just a darker shape now—a shadow to which DeWayne was painfully linked. The more he struggled, the more tightly Raffa held him. The smaller boy's eyes had begun to water from the pain. "Let me go," he begged through clenched teeth.

"I can't be alone in the dark and cold," said Raffa. "You're my best friend."

"Not if you keep hurting me," DeWayne said, getting angry.

The vise on his wrist tightened. "Best friends forever. *Forever.*"

The anger DeWayne was feeling suddenly melted into raw fear. With his free hand, he reached out frantically for the switch, found it, and flipped on the overhead light. The dazzling brightness confused Raffa momentarily. This caused him to loosen his grip long enough for DeWayne to twist free, though he nearly fell over, bumping into the wall. Not daring to pause, he blundered into the kitchen, slammed into the table, and knocked over the upset chair. Behind him, Raffa stumbled out of the room, kicking aside a chair that got in his way. DeWayne ran down the steps two at a time, nearly falling halfway. He heard the other boy thumping down the stairs—each step sounding as loud as a pile driver.

The deadbolt on the front door resisted DeWayne's frantic, fumbling fingers for a minute. Then, just as Raffa grabbed the sleeve of his shirt, he yanked the door open. There was a rip as a chunk of his school-uniform shirt came off in Raffa's hand. Then he was out the door, slamming it behind him.

DeWayne heard the other boy clumsily working the knob. But he had his key out and managed to unlock his own front door and bang it shut an instant before Raffa's fist crashed down on the solid wood panel with which his mother had replaced their own glass door following a series of neighborhood robberies.

DeWayne put his eye to the spy hole and saw Raffa standing there, a faraway look in his eyes, his fist rising and falling as he pounded on the door. "Best. Friends. Forever," he kept repeating, each syllable backed with a thunderous slam. "Best. Friends. *Forever.*"

"Get away, or I'm calling the police. I mean it. I'm calling 911 right now."

But the pounding continued. DeWayne wondered how long the door would hold. He picked up the hall phone and dialed the emergency number. "Someone is trying to get into the house to hurt me. He's my friend, but he's gone crazy."

The dispatcher quickly verified the address and promised that the police would be there in a matter of minutes.

The front door burst open. Heavy footsteps were coming down the hall as DeWayne fled to the kitchen at the back of the house. To his dismay, he realized his mother had double-locked the inner door between the kitchen and laundry room, as well as the outer door that led to the backyard.

Spinning like a trapped creature, he tried to decide what to do next. His own bedroom was a few feet away, but there was no lock on his door.

Suddenly it was too late. Raffa was shuffling through the doorway from the hall. His hand was outstretched, half pleading, half threatening: "Best friends *forever.*"

"*No way!*" screeched DeWayne. He picked up the first thing that came to hand: the Harry Potter book Raffa had given him the day before. Flinging it at the other boy's chest, he shouted, "*Let me alone!*"

The book hit Raffa with a *thump.* The boy looked down and picked up the book, its pages crumpled by the impact and the fall to the floor. He stared at it stupidly for a minute. Then, still holding the book, he backed into the shadowy hallway.

DeWayne, breathing heavily, clung to the kitchen counter, feeling as though he might just pass out. From far away, he heard the sound of police sirens. A moment later, there were shouts out the front, as two officers, guns drawn, pushed past the door that was hanging crookedly from twisted hinges.

There was no sign of Raffa. The crumpled book lay in the hall. After the officers had calmed DeWayne down and secured the lower flat, they cautiously went upstairs in search of the other boy. A few minutes later, they returned to report that the upstairs flat was empty.

They had just begun to question the boy about the afternoon's events, when Nikki Washington returned. "What on earth is going on? Oh, baby, are you all right?" she cried, gathering DeWayne in her arms.

"It was Raffa, Mama," DeWayne said, tears pouring down his cheeks. "He wanted to hurt me. I think he went crazy. And now he's gone. But I'm afraid he'll come back and try to hurt me again."

"Honey," she said, smoothing his hair, "I don't know what's been going on here, but Raffa couldn't have done this. Raffa couldn't hurt you even if he wanted to. I got a call at work just an hour ago. Raffa and his folks were killed this morning in a car crash near Fresno."

The Quilt

Her mother's disapproval of the quilt convinced Rebecca Jenkins that she had to have it. She was still angry that her parents had insisted she go along on their weekend drive to visit what seemed to the eleven-year-old girl like an endless round of antique stores and arts-and-crafts shops in Pennsylvania's Amish country. None of it interested her. To make peace, her mother had promised to let her pick out something for her room.

The curiously patterned quilt—alternating squares of red and black—was draped over a special frame in the front window of the arts-and-crafts store. Once inside the shop, which specialized in handsewn items, her mother tried in vain to direct Rebecca's eye to one or another of the more traditional quilts: gentle patterns in cheerful colors. But Rebecca ignored her mother and continued to study the curious example of some eccentric quilter's art.

With a sigh, Mrs. Jenkins, who knew a good deal about the art of quilting, asked the shopkeeper the price. She was shocked at the low figure the woman quoted for what was clearly an antique. "Has there been some mistake?"

"No," said the shopkeeper, a plump woman with her long gray hair pulled back into a ponytail. Then she thought further explanation was needed. "I've had it a long time—someone brought it in years ago and left it on consignment. They never came back. I've marked it down lots of times, but no one seems to be interested. Personally, I think the pattern is too strange. And the colors—well, you'd have a hard time finding the right place for it. Some people even find it *disturbing*."

While the women were talking, Rebecca went over to the window. A portion of the quilt hung down the back of the display frame. She reached out and touched one of the cloth squares: a block of red with swirls and stars and spirals of black thread that almost made her dizzy when she tried to sort out the overall design. When her fingers touched the cloth, she felt something like a faint electrical shock. She pulled her fingers back with a small cry.

"Are you all right?" her mother asked.

"Just static electricity, I guess," Rebecca answered.

The shopkeeper waddled over and began pulling the quilt from its frame. She laid it out on a counter so that the others could see the whole of it. Rebecca counted thirteen black panels at the center forming a star-burst design. Each was decorated with what might have been tiny letters sewn in black thread. She peered closely but couldn't be certain whether she was seeing actual words in a strange language or merely textures. Alternating squares of red and black—with a border of black edging—filled out the quilt.

Rebecca's mother ran a finger over the tiny stitches joining the individual squares and nodded appreciatively: "This is fine work." She looked at the backing, squeezed the padding, then decided, "It must be filled with cotton batting." But she still had misgivings. "Don't you want to look around some more?" she asked her daughter hopefully.

"I want this one," Rebecca said. "You promised."

Her mother shrugged and began to write a check. The saleswoman quickly folded and boxed the quilt. Mother and daughter went out into the town's sunny little main street to find Rebecca's father, who had gone in search of rare books. Then they began the long ride home to New Jersey.

The quilt didn't really match anything in Rebecca's room. Spread out on the bed, it overwhelmed the patterns in the braided rug and the curtains. But it was so dramatic in its red-and-black glory that the girl loved it. Her mother was less enthusiastic, though the skilled workmanship of the piece had made her more accepting. Smoothing a wrinkle, Rebecca felt again a little shock, much milder than what she had felt in the shop. Then a ripple seemed to run through the quilt, from under her hand to the center of the black star burst. For a moment the girl had the impression of something moving in the stuffing between the joined-together squares and the plain muslin backing. She immediately thought of horror movies where rats or spiders hid in or under things. She tugged the corner experimentally. Nothing. Rebecca laughed at her own foolishness.

That night Rebecca had a curious dream. In a large old-fashioned room lit by candles and the blaze in a stone fireplace, thirteen women dressed in red and black, wearing small lace caps, were holding a quilting bee. They sat around a large wooden frame hung on hooks from the rafters to waist height. On it, the quilt—her quilt—was stretched taut. The red and black cloth panels had been carefully basted to the backing, so the design could be clearly seen. The women were completing the quilt by sewing the panels into place with beautiful fine stitches. Rebecca, in her dream, seemed sometimes to float above the quilt, sometimes to stand between two of the women, who never noticed her. She watched, fascinated, as their needles fairly flew over the cloth. Much of the sewing was done in fancy patterns as well as straight lines: circles, stars, whorls, and zigzags. As they sewed, they repeated, in almost prayerlike fashion,

> *Fly, swift needle; bind sure thread:*
> *Stitch the world in black and red.*
> *Here are memories, there are dreams,*
> *Bound together by these seams.*
> *Past and present and what will be:*
> *Lost, then found, and finally free.*

*   *   *

Because she rarely remembered her dreams, Rebecca was surprised to find that when she woke up, she could recall all the details of this one. She even found the women's chant running through her brain like the catchphrase of a song that replays itself endlessly in one's head.

She had the same dream twice more. It felt like something she had lived through, it was so vivid. The faces of the women became familiar: some old, some middle-aged, two very young. They looked neither kind nor frightening—just absorbed by the needlework at hand. For them, there seemed to be nothing beyond the dipping and rising needles, the endlessly repeated chant.

She didn't mention the dream to her parents, sensing that in some vague way it would reinforce her mother's dislike of the quilt. But she recounted it in great detail to her friends Zoe and Amber after school one day. Zoe zoned out pretty quickly—far more interested in the upcoming soccer match against Davis Middle School, since she would be center midfielder. But Amber was really interested. "If there were thirteen of them," she said, lowering her voice to an excited whisper, "it could be a *coven*."

"I've heard that word," said Rebecca. "I just don't remember where."

"*Witches'* coven—duh!" Amber rolled her eyes in disbelief at her friend's ignorance. "Like in that movie, *Thirteen Witches*, we watched a couple of months ago at Tiffany's party? Where you had to guess which characters were witches and which weren't? Witches had these secret clubs—*covens*—where there had to be thirteen members."

26

The Quilt

"Oh, yeah. But it creeps me out to be dreaming junk like that."

"I think it's way cool. I wonder if your bedspread is haunted."

The idea seemed so silly, Rebecca laughed. "Get real!" But later, as she walked home from school, the idea seemed less silly. She remembered the little shocks she sometimes still got touching the quilt. When she got home, she ran her hand all over the spread, turned it over, did the same thing with the muslin underside—and found nothing. Not a lump or a wrinkle or anything unusual.

But, that night, she had a new dream. Again she seemed to walk and then to float around the candlelit, firelit room. The women worked with great urgency, sitting three and three and three and four on the sides of the quilting frame. The work Rebecca had seen begun in the first dream was now nearing completion. The oldest woman seemed to be the group's leader; she urged the others to work faster. Firelight flashed on the three gold bands she wore on the middle finger of her right hand. She led a chant that ran:

> *Fly, swift needle; bind sure thread:*
> *Stitch our fates in black and red.*
> *One will betray us,*
> *One tell our secrets,*
> *Then we'll sleep for a time*
> *Till one comes to free us.*

In this dream, Rebecca found herself drawn to the youngest of the group. She was sharp-faced, with frightened, darting eyes. The others didn't seem to notice her fear. But Rebecca saw her hands tremble so much that her sewing was flawed, leaving uneven spaces between the threads. The women on either side of her scolded her, then picked out the imperfect stitches and watched to be sure matters were corrected with the second pass of the young woman's needle. Her hands continued to shake, dream-Rebecca saw, but the woman forced herself to stay calm and her fingers to obey.

Now the oldest one was repeating over and over only the words:

> *One will betray us,*
> *One tell our secrets.*

The others paused to watch her as she plied her needle. "Mother Quigby," asked one of the middle-aged women, "tell us who the traitor is, if you know."

"It matters not," murmured the old woman. "What's done can't be undone. What's to happen will come about. The work is important. See to the work. Let the traitor see to her own fate." With a collective sigh, the others around the frame bent to their sewing.

Suddenly, with a sob, the youngest got up and ran off, throwing open the door to vanish into the night beyond. Several of the younger women rose as though they would follow her, but Mother Quigby, raising her hand with its three gold rings, commanded them, "Stop! Finish the work at hand. It alone is our hope. Sister Rowena does not know the true meaning of our work. So her betrayal will not be complete."

The Quilt

As Rebecca watched unseen, their hands raced to complete the quilt. Needles moving with blurring speed, the final precious stitches were finished. A moment later, Mother Quigby, her three rings blazing red-gold in the fire's glow, cut the last thread and announced, "It's done. Now." She stretched her hands out. The twelve linked hands in a circle around the quilt. They chanted strange words, meaningless to dream-Rebecca, who felt like a cloud hovering near the ceiling, or a breeze passing among the women. Once or twice, she was sure old Mother Quigby looked across at her and nodded. But the woman never indicated to the others that there was a secret watcher in the room.

Mother Quigby had each woman lean forward and touch a hand to one of the thirteen black squares of the dark star burst at the center. When they did, there was a flash—not of light, but of darkness, which seemed to drink in all the light in the room. The candles shrank to pinpricks of light; the fire, to a pool of soft glow. Rebecca felt a weight crushing her, so that the air was squeezed out of her lungs. But the sensation passed. Then the candles flared and the fireplace blazed—but the room was empty, save for the quilt, swaying slightly on its suspended frame.

Where had the women gone? Rebecca wondered. Then the door of the cabin flung open. Men in old-fashioned doublets and hats and leather or cotton pants burst into the room. They carried lanterns and torches. Among the last to enter, clinging to the arm of one handsome young man, was Rowena.

"Hags!" voices cried. "Where have you hidden yourselves?" They searched the cupboards, beneath the quilt, even the window seat, which hadn't space enough to hide the smallest child.

The men had closed the door behind them, but a sudden wind slammed it open, howling into the room. It swirled around, causing the candles to flicker and the fire to flare. Then lifting the quilt, the wind ripped it loose from its frame and sent it billowing around the room like some living thing. The men drew swords and hacked at the cloth, as they cried, "Deviltry!" and "Witchery!" But the whirlwind kept the black-and-red cloth dancing away from their blades, wrapping it briefly around one or another of the invaders. Then, suddenly, the wind swept the quilt away into the darkness outside. Rebecca, feeling light as a feather, was pulled along after the escaping quilt into the night. For a moment she saw it flying like a living thing beneath the full moon. She reached for it, arms outstretched, feeling an overwhelming desire to catch it, but it skittered away into the darkness before her.

Abruptly, Rebecca felt herself sinking earthward, toward a swell that suddenly became the roof of a house. She recognized her home in Lincoln Park, New Jersey. She drifted gently through the roof and down toward the bed, where she saw herself sleeping under the red-and-black quilt.

Then her alarm went off, she was awake in her own bed, and it was morning. The quilt was neatly folded at the foot of her bed. Since she had fallen asleep cuddled under its thickness, she guessed that her mother had folded down the spread after she'd drifted off. Sunlight streamed through the window. But she felt as tired as if she hadn't slept at all.

The Quilt

In her half-awake state, she thought she heard dream voices calling her name—but they were drowned out by her mother's very real voice warning her that she'd be late for school if she didn't get a move on.

Amber, whose locker was next to hers, asked, "Are you wearing different liner or blush or something? You look different."

"No."

"Well, you look thinner. Wish I could look thinner." Amber ran her hands down her ample hips and sighed.

"I haven't been sleeping well," Rebecca said. "I've been having crazy dreams."

"Maybe I should watch those all-night horror movies on Channel 10. They'd keep me awake," said Amber. "Then I could lose weight, same as you."

"*I'm not losing weight.* I'm just tired this morning," Rebecca insisted.

"Whatever," said Amber, who clearly didn't believe a word.

"Are you all right, hon?" her mother asked at breakfast two days later. "You look a little peaked."

"*I'm fine!*"

But when she looked in the mirror, she saw that her face looked thinner, sharper. She felt weak at times, and her eyes darted about in a haunted, restless way. Often she imagined she heard her name whispered so faintly it seemed unreal. *Am I going crazy?* she wondered.

It was only when she hugged the quilt in her arms, or lay with it pulled up to her chin, that she felt good again.

Saying she wasn't feeling well, she stayed home more and more from school. She talked less and less on the phone to her friends. Her mother and father asked what was wrong, but she shrugged them off. Watching them watching her, Rebecca felt that they were all becoming strangers to one another. She was becoming a stranger to *herself*: she hardly recognized her face in the mirror—looking more pinched and fearful with every glance.

She sat for hours, staring out the window, the quilt wrapped around her. She often had waking dreams, in which the old woman, Mother Quigby, visited her. Rebecca could see her mouth moving, talking to her; but all the girl could hear were sighs and whispers, too faint to understand.

At first the woman had appeared in the far corner of Rebecca's room, but each time the dream returned, Mother Quigby was a step closer. And each step, Rebecca felt, brought her closer to learning the meaning of the other's visits.

"I've made an appointment with the doctor for tomorrow," her mother was saying.

Rebecca hadn't been aware that her mother had come into her room. She'd been dozing and waking in her chair, wrapped in the quilt. Startled, she saw that Mother Quigby had followed her out of her dream into wakefulness. The old woman, faint enough to see through, stood only a few paces away. Rebecca rubbed her eyes. Her mother was standing right in front of her, arms folded, looking angry and worried. Just behind her stood Mother Quigby, a figure of air and darkness, her own arms folded, as if mocking the other woman. Rebecca's mother followed her daughter's eyes, turned—and saw nothing. She turned back and asked, "What are you staring at?"

Rebecca remembered how, in her earliest dreams, she had stood near or hovered above the women working on the quilt, and none saw her, except Mother Quigby. Had her own life become a dream? Was Mother Quigby the sleeper who was dreaming this room and Rebecca and her mother? The girl felt more and more confused.

"Becky, you're frightening me—you look so strange," said her mother. "Should I call a doctor now?" She put out a hand to feel whether the girl had a fever.

"Don't touch me!" Rebecca snarled, pulling back. Behind her mother, the old woman nodded. Rebecca drew the quilt close around her. "Leave us alone!"

"What are you talking about?" asked her mother, looking around, seeing nothing. "Who else do you think is here?"

The quilt was warm. But it also seemed charged with a power now. She could feel something like electricity flowing through it, flowing into her. The old woman was smiling, watching eagerly to see what the girl would do.

Her mother reached forward again. "You must have a fever."

"*Get out!*" Rebecca ordered. The quilt was crackling with energy. Her mother pulled back her hand with a cry, as though she'd touched an electrical wire. The curtains at the window began to flap as though driven by a powerful wind, though the window was shut. It was barely noon, but the windows reflected the red of sunset and the blackness of night in alternating panes. "Get out *now!*" Rebecca stood up, the black-and-red quilt wrapped around her like a cloak.

Her startled mother was pushed roughly toward the door as though by dozens of invisible hands. She beat her hands against the air and wailed, "They're pinching me! Make them stop!" But she was forced back, as Rebecca watched silently and the old woman nearly doubled over with silent laughter.

The door was yanked open, her mother was thrust into the hall, and the door slammed behind her. There was a soft *click* as an unseen hand turned the key in the lock.

"Rebecca! Open this door at once! What is going on?" her mother called. But her voice was muffled, not only by the closed door, but as though it were coming across a vast distance. The curtains dropped back into place as the mysterious wind died away. But the window remained a checkerboard of red and black panes.

The old woman, still half-transparent, was speaking. For the first time, Rebecca understood her words: "Place the quilt upon the bed."

Unwilling to give up the quilt's warmth and power, but more frightened of disobeying Mother Quigby, Rebecca did as she was told, smoothing the material out. "Good! Good!" the woman said eagerly. She was standing on the other side of the bed.

> *Snip, swift scissors, cut the thread:*
> *Loose the world in black and red.*

34

The Quilt

Here the memories, here the dreams,
Hidden deep within these seams.
The waiting now is past and done:
The promised end is finally won.

"What do I do now?" asked Rebecca.

But the old woman just repeated the verse as she faded from view. Rebecca stared at the quilt, then at the spot where the old woman had stood. At last she understood. Ignoring the faint beating on her door and her mother's muffled cries, Rebecca went to the top drawer of her dresser and took out a pair of nail scissors. Gently she began to cut the fine stitches holding together the thirteen black squares of cloth at the center of the quilt.

As soon as she'd snipped the final thread, a withered hand, its middle finger banded with three gold rings, thrust up, clawed into the light. The eldest of the twelve dream quilters began pulling herself free.

"I greet thee, Rebecca, our destined thirteenth sister," said Mother Quigby.

In silent answer, Rebecca stretched out her hands to steady and welcome the first of the reborn women.

Circus Dreams

Circus
Friday & Saturday
Two Days Only!

The event was announced on posters that appeared overnight on telephone poles, on fences, and in store windows throughout the town of Redwood Cove, a hamlet snuggled on the rocky shore of northern California. The words were printed in gray letters, outlined in black, on a yellow square of plastic. The name of the circus was Dreamtime, and the setting was the meadow between the town and the Coast Junior College campus, which overlooked the Pacific.

Chaz Farris and his best (and only) friend, Billy Evans, rode their bikes over there Saturday morning to check things out. They watched the workers raise the steel frame for the main tent and set up the sideshows. "Those guys are called roustabouts," Chaz informed his friend.

"'Kay," said Billy, who took his friend's showing off about knowing the proper word for circus laborers in stride. Chaz read all the time. Billy had warned him once that he might burn his brain out from overloading it with too much information. But whereas Billy was cool about it, the other third-graders regarded Chaz's endless reading and adult vocabulary as positive proof of his "weirdness."

Laying their bikes side by side a short distance away, the boys watched as the men sweating in the hot sun draped the gray canvas tent over the metal uprights and cross-beams. Growing bored, they checked out the ponies in their pen beneath a striped orange-and-white awning. Circular tracks were set out for a Tilt-a-Whirl and humped tracks for a roller coaster, which Chaz and Billy agreed looked as though it wouldn't excite anyone beyond first grade.

What interested Chaz most was the "Wonders of the Weird World" exhibit. Three trailers were linked together, with a canvas extension along the front doubling the size of the place. A red-framed canvas flap served as a door. Ads painted on either side of it promised "A Sideshow of Curiosities and Horrors" and "Sights Guaranteed to Feed Your Dreams and Fan Your Nightmares." This interested Chaz far more than the rides, the games, the ponies, or the main tent. He watched crates and boxes and barrels being carried in, imagining what sort of things—beautiful or unnerving—they contained.

But when he asked his parents to take him, they refused. "It's nothing but a trash show," his mother said. "Not a proper circus."

"You'd probably have your pocket picked," his father said, "or get food poisoning from the junk food there."

"Billy's going," Chaz said stubbornly.

"That's up to his parents," said his mother. "Don't argue."

Billy went to the Dreamtime Circus on Friday night. He reported what he had seen to Chaz on Saturday morning, as he lobbed rocks at a bird's nest high in a tree. Chaz was mowing the lawn in front of his house. "It wasn't a very good circus," Billy said. "There weren't any animals except the ponies. Some guy jumped on a trampoline. A guy and a girl did some tricks on the trapeze. The juggler dropped most of his pins. The clowns were corny. And there was a girl who kept a lot of Hula-Hoops going—but anyone could do that."

"Did you look at the 'Wonders of the Weird World'?"

"Nah, I was pretty bored after the show. Besides, my folks let me play so many games and ride so many rides, they didn't want to pay for anything else."

"I'd have gone there first."

"Shoot—you'd probably just see some girl dressed up like a fake mermaid and a bunch of old dishes someone said were from India or Egypt." Billy lowered his voice as though he were about to share a deep secret. "I'll tell you the only good part of the circus is when it's gone."

"What do you mean?"

"Meet me at my house on Sunday morning after church and you'll see," said Billy with a mysterious smile.

On Sunday Chaz went over to Billy's house. There the other boy proudly displayed the metal detector he'd bought with money from his paper route and allowance. "I got it at the army surplus store," Billy explained. "It's an old model, but it works." Chaz stared doubtfully at the metal disk, the size of a small garbage-can lid, attached to one end of a rod, with a control box at the other end. A wire wrapped around the rod, connecting disk and box. A grip like a backward bike handle allowed Billy to hold the thing in front of him, while a pair of headphones would let him listen for the telltale pinging that would signal found metal. "People drop all sorts of things at places like the circus," Billy told his friend. "Coins and jewelry and junk. This could make me rich."

Intrigued, Chaz followed his friend to the now-empty field near the junior college. The Dreamtime Circus had been pulled down, packed up, and moved out overnight. The only sign that it had been there at all was the crushed grass all around and the empty popcorn boxes and half-eaten caramel apples.

Chaz kept looking at the space where the "Wonders of the Weird World" display had been, but only a fast-fading rectangle of flattened grass and a few postholes indicated it had ever been there. Billy got to work, moving up and down the field, swinging the detector from side to side in long sweeping arcs—like someone working a weed-whacker, Chaz thought, as he trailed behind. In an hour, Billy had found a child's ring (junky, with a pink plastic flower instead of a jewel), a rosary, and ten dollars and twenty-three cents in coins. Satisfied with the haul, he suggested they go downtown and invest some of the coins in a couple of games at the arcade.

"I'd like to try using the detector," said Chaz.

"It's getting hot, and I'm tired of this."

"Let me keep it for a while. I'll bring it back later today."

"I just got it," Bill objected.

"I'll take good care of it," Chaz promised. "Hey! We're best friends. You know you can trust me."

Impatient to get to the arcade, Billy turned over the detector, then rode off on his bike. Chaz made a few experimental sweeps with the thing, then began moving in a pattern the way Billy had. But all he turned up was a couple of soda cans, a long piece of scrap metal, and a set of house keys without a name. He threw the cans away, not wanting to bother lugging them to the recycling area at the far end of town. He pocketed the keys in case somebody posted a reward for their return. Later he found a quarter and three pennies, but that was all.

The day grew hotter. What little breeze there was from the ocean died away. He abandoned the side-to-side exploration of the field, walking across to the space where the "Wonders of the Weird World" had stood. He began sweeping the detector carefully over the space.

Halfway along, he heard the *pingpingping* that signaled

a find. Expecting it to be a crushed soda can or other junk, he was surprised to see a small patch of recently dug earth. The steady pinging insisted that there was metal underneath. Clearly, someone had buried something. A forgotten cashbox? He wondered. Or something gross? Curious, he switched off the control box, set the detector down, and began digging with his fingers.

The earth was dry and crumbly and easy to work through. About a foot down, his fingertips touched the metal lid of a container about the size of a shoebox. Eagerly he pulled it up. It did look like a cashbox. It was old and made of dull, dented metal, like heavy tin. The lid seemed to have been jammed on tightly, then sealed with something that looked like red wax. He shook it slightly, felt something inside shift softly, and almost thought, for a minute, that he heard faint scratching under the lid. *Could there be some animal inside?* But there were no air holes; when he listened again, he heard nothing. He decided it was only his imagination at work.

He scraped the wax away. It was sticky and clung to his fingernails like nail polish—or, he thought, *blood*. He wiped his fingers clean on his jeans, which were heading for the next wash anyway. Then he tried to pry up the lid, but it wouldn't give. He looked around for some tool, then he remembered the piece of scrap metal he'd tossed aside earlier. When he found it again, he began working at the lid. He didn't notice the three boys on bicycles riding across the field toward him.

"Hey, it's Chaz the spaz!" yelled Scott Beecham, one of

Chaz's least favorite people. He was followed by Tony Escalante and Dennis Graf, two other losers. "What's that?" asked Scott, breaking to a halt, using one leg to balance himself and his bike. He picked up the metal detector.

"Give it back! It's not mine."

"You got that right!" said Scott. "It's mine now."

Chaz stood uncertainly, unwilling to set the metal box down for fear that one of the other boys, who were on either side of him, would grab it, too. "What's in the box?" asked Dennis, making a snatch for it. Chaz took a step back, put his foot in the freshly dug hole, and fell over backward. The box and scrap metal went spinning into the air, both hitting the ground with soft *thunks.*

"Spaz-man!" yelled Scott. He wheeled off on his bike, waving the metal detector over his head like a warrior holding a spear. The other boys followed, whipping through the recovering grass like mini-tornadoes.

"Come back!" Chaz yelled halfheartedly. He knew there wasn't a chance Scott would abandon his prize. A minute later, the three boys were on the road that ran alongside the field and racing toward town.

"Great! Just great!" muttered Chaz. He dreaded confessing to Billy that he'd lost the metal detector. He wondered how much a replacement would cost, since he doubted that Scott would ever give back his prize. Maybe if Chaz got his father to confront Scott, his dad could get it back. Of course, Scott and his pals would then brand him a "tattletail" and a "crybaby." Whatever he did, he was going to come out the loser.

He decided to put off telling Billy or his father for a while. He turned his attention to the tin box. He was able to jam the thin end of the metal piece between the lid and one side of the box. Using it like a lever, he finally managed to pop the cover free.

It was full of salt. Why would someone bury a tin box of salt? he wondered. He pushed a finger in and felt something. He poured out the salt.

There was a horrible doll underneath. At least, he thought it was a doll at first. Ugly, hairy, brown, eyes closed. Spindly arms crossed on the chest. But only the top half looked like a furry human: the bottom half was a fish. It was like he was staring at the dried-up body of a tiny mermaid. A real mermaid. But there was something wrong about it. Half–grossed-out, he touched his finger to where the hairy upper half of the body was joined to the dried fishy part, which felt as hard as wood. He discovered a line of very fine stitches hidden by the brown hair, which hung below the waist.

It was a fake. Clearly someone had sewn together part of a monkey and a big fish. Up close, the fakiness was clear. But, Chaz thought, if you put the thing in a glass case with the right lighting, it would look real. It must have come from the "Wonders of the Weird World." If this was a fake, probably most of the stuff they'd had on display had been, too. So maybe he hadn't missed much.

Shaking free the last of the salt, he lifted the monkeyfish out of its box. In the sunlight, the twisted mouth that had looked so grim a moment before seemed now to be grinning.

He poured out the last of the salt carefully to be sure there was nothing else in the box. There wasn't.

He decided that someone at the sideshow had gotten tired of the thing. Or maybe a customer had called it a fake. But why bury it? Why not throw it in a garbage can and be done with it? Maybe they were afraid the A.S.P.C.A. or those animal rights people would want to know where it had come from, whether someone at the circus was hurting animals. But the thing looked old to Chaz—like something that belonged in a real museum. In any case, it was his now. He'd keep it, but he wouldn't tell his parents, he decided. He could hear his mother ordering him to "throw that disgusting thing away this instant!"

But he'd show Billy. . . .

Except seeing Billy meant admitting that he'd lost the metal detector—not something he was ready to face just yet. He put the monkey-fish back in the tin box and set off for home.

His father was working in the garage; his mother was out. Chaz took the box to his bedroom, took one more look at the hideous contents, and put it far back in the closet under a stack of games and puzzles.

The phone rang in the hall. "Farris residence," he answered.

"Where's my metal detector?" Billy demanded.

"Um, I gotta go run some errands for my dad right now," said Chaz. "I'll bring it by later,"

"When?"

"Before dinner."

"'Kay. Bye."

Chaz lay down on the bed, trying to decide what to do. Tell his father? Hunt for Scott and the others and try to beg or bribe them to give back the detector? But he had only a dollar and the change he'd found in the field. And he doubted his father would give him an advance on his allowance. He might stall Billy a little longer, but what good would that do?

The room was filled with warm late-afternoon sun. He began to drift off to sleep. In a half-dream, he was back at the circus field, being taunted by the three other boys, led by a detector-waving Scott. He could feel anger flooding him at their cries of "Spaz-man!" He could almost hear the sneering laughter of his enemies. There was also a faint scratching that sounded like a mouse in a wall somewhere. But all he could focus on was the hateful laughs and hated faces of the other boys. Then the shadow of something towering behind him fell across the scene, blotting out the other boys' faces, drowning out their laughter, which seemed to be turning to shouts. In the dream, he was glad to know they were scared (they had been so mean to him), but he didn't want to look around and see what was causing the shadow, what was terrifying them so. Their faces grew dimmer, their shouts fainter. There was only thick shadow everywhere, as Chaz fell into a deeper, dreamless sleep.

His father shook him awake. "Dinner, lazybones." Chaz sat up suddenly. He looked at the clock. He'd been asleep almost two hours. He'd had some kind of nightmare but couldn't remember any of it.

The phone rang. His father went to answer it, with an added, "Hurry up—food's on."

With a sinking feeling, Chaz guessed it was Billy. It was. He took the phone from his father. "We just got finished doing some work," he said quickly. "Now I have to eat dinner. I'll bring it by after supper."

"You better," was all Billy said.

Chaz picked at his food, until his mother and father gradually pried the story of the lost detector out of him. They seemed to think he'd been careless to lose it in the first place, but his father agreed to go over to the Beecham house that evening and demand that Scott return the item. However, he insisted that Chaz come with him. The boy could just imagine the insults that Scott and his friends would sling at him the next day for involving parents in what should have been a boys-only dispute.

At least Billy wouldn't be mad at him. This mattered most of all, because Chaz had no other real friend.

But what happened at the Beecham house didn't solve anything. The sheriff's car was parked in front. Chaz's father pulled in behind it. Scott's little sisters, looking frightened, were holding hands on the porch swing. "Stay put," his father ordered. Chaz leaned out the window and tried to find out what was going on. Sheriff Nicholson stepped out from behind the screen door and talked briefly with his father. (Chaz recognized the man who had come to his school to talk about the dangers of drug use.) Then the sheriff went back inside, while Mr. Farris returned to the car. "Scott hasn't come home," he told Chaz. "And a couple of his friends are missing, too. When did you see them?"

"I'm not sure exactly. Maybe around two, when Scott took the detector."

"Apparently they were riding their bikes near Stony Point Park about 5 P.M. That's the last anybody's seen them. Knowing that bunch, they're probably up to no good."

Unwilling to face Billy in person, Chaz decided to call him. Over Billy's cries of "Why'd you let 'em take it?" he explained that he'd tried to get it back and that his father had promised to help him. But matters would have to wait until the missing boys were found.

"You really are a spaz," was the last thing Billy said before he slammed down the phone.

Feeling almost sad enough to cry, Chaz hung up, thinking that nothing could be worse than having his only friend mad at him.

But the next day, things got worse. The missing boys were found at the bottom of the Stony Point headlands. The smashed remains of the detector were found under Scott's body. The three had apparently fallen to their deaths while playing too close to the drop-off. It was only after rescue workers brought up the bodies that word spread that they had been badly scratched and clawed before they died. There was talk around town that they had been attacked by wild dogs. The animals had been plaguing the park and other open areas all summer—even coming into town to raid garbage cans. The metal detector might have been used in a hopeless attempt to fight off the animals. In trying to fight their way free, the popular theory went, the boys had somehow lost track of how close they were to the drop to the boulders below.

Chaz, who was afraid of heights, found himself imagining the terror of the boys' fatal plunge. He remembered the awful time he had frozen partway up a hillside on a Boy Scout hike and had to be rescued by park rangers. That feeling of terror—can't climb higher, can't back down—had become a joke that hadn't stopped with his Scout troop. Soon the whole school had known what a coward he was. He didn't like Scott and his friends—in fact, yesterday he had *hated* them—but he felt sorry about what had happened. No one should have such an awful death: spinning into air with nothing to catch onto and the hungry rocks waiting below.

Chaz avoided Billy, who he knew would have heard about the ruined metal detector from the stories in the papers or on TV. But while he was riding his bike late in the day, he passed Billy and several other kids walking near the arcade.

"You owe me a new metal detector!" shouted Billy. Chaz, his face burning, just pedaled away as fast as he could. But he could hear Billy yelling, "Run away, you big baby! You're still gonna have to pay!" Now all the other kids were yelling, too; fortunately, distance quickly muffled their insults.

But there was no real escape. Shortly before dinner two nights later, Billy and his father—in a strange replay of the

visit Chaz and his father had made to the Beecham house—
rang the Farrises' front doorbell. While Billy smirked, his
father—a jerk and a loudmouth as far as Chaz was concerned—insisted that he wanted payment *on the spot* for the
smashed detector. He shouted down Chaz's father's argument that the other boys had stolen it from his son and that
they, not Chaz, were responsible for the loss.

"Chaz promised me he'd take care of it," Billy whined.

In the end, while the two adults glared at each other,
Chaz's father wrote out a check for the full amount. Billy,
standing beside his father, managed to shoot Chaz a lot of
self-satisfied smiles. Chaz found himself *hating* his former
friend. He wanted to punch the smile off his face.

Following his father out of the house, Billy turned just
for a moment to whisper, "Spaz-man, you are *king* of the
spazzes!"

Chaz's father slammed the door behind the two. "That
money is coming out of your allowance," he said, rubbing his
neck. "And don't go borrowing anyone's things ever again."

Chaz shrugged. Billy had turned traitor on him. His
father's anger meant little considering the rage he felt
against the other boy. He knew that, with Billy against him,
the days ahead were going to be long and very lonely.
Feeling equal parts anger and self-pity, he went to his room.
A thought crossed his mind: maybe he could sell the monkey-
fish to one of the antique dealers in town. There were plenty
of shops that made money off the many tourists who came
to the area. But when he lifted it out of the box and looked
at it, he decided that no one would give him more than a

few bucks for such an ugly old thing. He'd never make enough to pay his father back and get him off his case. Back into its closet hiding place went the monkey-fish's tin box. Then Chaz got ready for bed.

In bed, he tried to read one of the library books on natural history he'd checked out weeks ago. But none of the books that had looked so fascinating on the library shelves interested him now. He let each one, hardly sampled, drop to the floor.

His mind was filled with images of Billy's face as the other said, "Spaz-man, you are *king* of the spazzes!" The scene kept playing over and over in his mind. He wished he could fall asleep, but he was so angry, he could feel his heart beating away. He kept making his hands into fists as he imagined pounding Billy—one punch for every smirk earlier that night.

He heard a *scritchscritchscritch* and realized the mouse was back. He could hear it near the closet. Or was it in the closet? The sound was too faint for him to be sure. He got his flashlight and checked along the wall outside the closet and searched carefully inside, among scattered shoes and stacked games; but he could find no trace of a hole or droppings. Listening intently, he could hear nothing. But when he shut off the lights and lay back down, he was sure he heard faint scratching. He would mention it to his father in the morning.

But as soon as his head hit the pillow and sleep came to claim him, Billy's smug face appeared, mouthing *spazspazspaz* like a mosquito's relentless buzz in his ears. Chaz clamped his hands to the sides of his head, but he couldn't shut out the hateful words that were playing inside his brain. He didn't know when he'd fallen asleep. He sensed only that he had shifted into a nightmare world where Billy led a chorus of grinning faces in name calling, until Chaz's rage blended with the huge shadow of something behind him that grew and grew until it swallowed up the whole of his dream and stopped the cruel voices forever.

When he woke up, he couldn't remember anything, except that he'd tossed and turned all night long.

His parents were silent at the breakfast table. That was fine: he didn't want to talk to them either. He didn't want to talk to *anyone*. He didn't run into Billy the next day—or anyone else. He stayed close to the house, reading, putting together old jigsaw puzzles from deep inside his closet, barely speaking to his parents—or they to him. At dinner, things were as tense as the summer air before a thunderstorm broke over the town.

It wasn't until the next day, when he was returning the latest library books, that the librarian said, "Isn't it awful? They still haven't found a trace."

"Of what?"

She seemed startled by his response. "Why, I'm talking about your friend, Billy Evans. I know the two of you used to come in here pretty often. Now he's disappeared."

"We're not friends anymore," said Chaz. "I didn't know anything happened to him."

"You should pay attention to the news," the woman said. "He's been gone two days now. The sheriff's department suspects *foul play*," she added dramatically. "I must say, those other boys getting chewed up and falling off the head-lands, and now this—well, it just seems *odd*, if you ask me."

Chaz pedaled his bike home deep in thought. Things were rattling around the back of his mind like the pieces of a jigsaw puzzle where you saw bits of color and pattern—but couldn't quite get a handle on the whole picture.

No trace of Billy was found. The sheriff came around and asked Chaz about the last time he had seen Billy, but when Chaz reported that it had been the day when Billy came over with his father, the sheriff lost interest. What-ever had happened had happened long after that.

There was talk of kidnapping, but Chaz was sure Billy was dead. He couldn't say why he was sure, but he sensed it was true. For several nights his sleep was troubled with visions of Billy, chased by something big and shadowy, running through the woods. In his dream, Chaz heard the pursuer. It made a slithery sound amid the crackling of trees and bushes as they were shoved aside by the thing's size.

He often woke up to the whispery mouse scratching. He had told his father, who had put out traps but hadn't caught anything.

The other kids in town avoided him. He felt more of an outcast than ever: *king of the spazzes.* Their dislike made him angry with himself. No one liked him—even his best friend had turned on him—because he *was* a spaz, he decided. He couldn't imagine going back to school in September with the kids who detested him. They hung together and pointed and whispered and giggled and ran off if he came near. He called his image in the mirror names like *Spaz!* and *Creep!*

The unhappier he was with himself, the more his dreams turned confused and frightening. In them, Billy and Scott and Tony and Dennis were yelling at him from across a vast dark space, but he couldn't understand what they were saying. Sometimes he thought they were making fun, sometimes he thought they were warning him about some danger.

Billy was never found, though an Amber Alert—a statewide kidnapping alert—had been put out.

Chaz stayed in his room much of the time. The mouse continued to scratch in the closet, though it never left a trace. Chaz began to think of the unseen creature as the only one (except his parents) who wanted to be near him. What was left of the summer had soured. More and more he blamed himself for being so unpopular, so unhappy, so fearful about returning to school after Labor Day. The year ahead loomed as sheer misery.

Then one night lightning from a summer thunderstorm blew a power pole transformer and plunged much of Redwood Cove—including his own house—into darkness. Chaz was alone that evening; his parents were next door visiting. He could see flickering candlelight in the windows there. Because power outages were pretty common, his father had scattered battery-powered lanterns throughout the house. Chaz had set one on his bureau, beside the mirror, to magnify the light.

The phone rang; it was his mother calling to be sure he was all right and to assure him they'd be home in half an hour. "I'm fine," he said.

He went back to his room and leaned his elbows on the edge of the bureau and stared at his pale reflection. He was always telling them he was fine, when *nothing* about himself or his life was okay. Everything was a stupid mess. Somehow, he was to blame for the mess. "Spaz!" he shouted to his reflection as it shouted back at him. "Dumb, stupid spaz. No one likes you. They hate you! I hate you!" He began to cry and grew angrier at the weepy wuss across from him. He punched his fist into the glass, grimly satisfied at the pain that flared in his knuckles—as if hurting himself was somehow hurting the hateful image across from him.

Something small *scritched* in the closet; something bigger shifted. Something scratched loudly on the inside wall. Something *slithered*. With a click the closet door unlatched itself, then swung open, hitting the wall with a soft *thunk*. He was suddenly too afraid to turn around, to move, to breathe. Staring straight ahead into the mirror, he could see, over his reflected shoulder, a huge shape filling the closet door, a strange black shadow rippling against the familiar darkness, blotting out the shapes of hanging coats and pants and sweaters. It shouldered aside the hanger bar; it knocked the shelves above off their brackets as the thing grew.

In an instant, he understood. The monkey-fish had been buried in the field because someone was *afraid* of its power. Maybe the salt and red wax were some kind of voodoo to hold the wicked magic inside. It was an *evil* thing, he was sure. With a moan that was half fear, half regret, Chaz realized what he had done. He had hated Scott and Tony and Dennis, and they had died. He had hated Billy, and Billy had disappeared. Somehow the thing he had let free had done awful things to people he hated.

And now he hated *himself.*

"I don't, I don't *really!*" he and his reflection whispered to each other.

But they weren't very good liars, either of them.

Behind them both, the shadow slithered closer.

Rosalie

Shortly after the twins Maryjo and Suellen had celebrated their thirteenth birthday, curious things began to happen in the Jarvie household. Doors slammed when no one was near. The microwave turned itself on. The television blared suddenly. The upstairs shower started running. Pots and pans rattled in the cupboards. Lights flickered on and off. Silverware flew off a table, a clock jumped off a wall, and a package of Chips Ahoy! dropped from the counter. Lady, the family's cocker spaniel, would sometimes growl at a corner of the room, as though she sensed something no one else could see. This, to the family, was the most unnerving part of the haunting—or whatever it was.

The twins' mother taught at the local high school; their

father worked as an accountant at the community college campus. Both parents had read enough and talked to enough knowledgeable people to suspect that this was a result of "poltergeist" —noisy ghost—activity. At first they thought the twins might be playing tricks (something the girls had done from time to time), but things happened when neither Maryjo nor Suellen was around.

Alan Jarvie even called upon someone from the college psychology department, Dr. Claude Morris, whose specialty was strange happenings—like "poltergeist effects," as he called them. He paid several visits to the house, interviewed the parents and the twins at great length, and even saw a crystal candlestick slide across the dining room table and shatter on the floor when no one else was in the room. "This is a case of RSPK—recurrent spontaneous psychokinesis," Dr. Morris told the family one evening when everyone had gathered in the living room.

"What's that?" Maryjo blurted out.

The professor smiled. "Psychokinesis, or PK, means the power of the mind to move things. There's a theory that the human body has an energy field around it that—in rare instances—can move move small objects or even furniture, break windows, even start fires." He paused to wipe his glasses, then continued, "There have been well-documented cases throughout history. Usually the activity is triggered unconsciously by a teenager who is under a lot of tension or stress." He smiled at Maryjo and Suellen. "And here you have two perfect candidates. I've never encountered a situation where twins were involved. Maybe they're doubling the power."

The girls looked at each other and made faces. They were aware of their parents looking at them in a funny way.

"I'm not tense," said Maryjo.

"I don't feel stressed," added Suellen.

"It might be nothing more than the fact that you're both growing up. You've just become teenagers. Your bodies are changing; life is changing." Dr. Morris shrugged. "It's hard to say."

"Is there anything we can do to stop this?" asked Ellen Jarvie.

"The activity usually fades away on its own," he said. "I'd like to keep in touch with you about this. Strange as it seems, what you're experiencing is certainly unusual, but by no means unique." He got up to go, and the older Jarvies walked him to the door.

As soon as the adults were gone, Maryjo said to Suellen, "Wouldn't it be cool if he was right and we could move things the way he said? Let's try, right now. Let's both think about making the coffee table move."

But though they both stared at the table and tried to think it into shifting around, nothing happened.

"Bummer," said Maryjo, giving up.

Suellen wrinkled her nose. "I think the guy was just making it up so he wouldn't have to tell Mom and Dad he didn't know what's really happening."

Whatever the cause, things started to happen more often—not less, as Dr. Morris had suggested. Pictures fell off the wall. A coffee cup flew across the kitchen, just missing

Rosalie

Ellen Jarvie. Smoke alarms sounded without any cause. Lady continued to growl and snarl at unseen things.

In desperation, the Jarvies, thinking it might calm things, invited the pastor of their church in to bless the house. But things remained unchanged after the prayers and the blessing.

One rainy afternoon, when the girls were left alone briefly while their parents went shopping, Maryjo, who was playing with a Game Boy, said to Suellen, who was reading, "I know what's making all the weird stuff happen."

Not looking up, Suellen said, "Sure, it's that psycho-whatever stuff."

"No, it's not," her sister said. "It's a ghost—the ghost of a little girl named Rosalie who used to live in this house, and died here. She's just playing. She's lonely."

Suellen carefully put a bookmark in place before she answered. "Then she plays mean. She almost hit Mom with a coffee cup the other day."

"Oh, she can be a brat," said Maryjo. "But she doesn't want to hurt anyone, *really*."

"Well, I wish she'd go play someplace else. Mom and Dad are getting really tired of this stuff. I heard them arguing the other day. Mom wants to sell the house. Dad doesn't." She cupped her hands around her mouth. "Hey, Rosalie! Get lost! Go haunt some other family."

"She's not here," said Maryjo.

"How can you tell, if she's invisible?"

"Look at Lady." The dog was asleep near the heating vent. "Lady always knows when Rosalie's around."

"Have you told Mom and Dad?"

"They wouldn't believe me. They're always saying we've got too much imagination for our own good." Maryjo lowered her voice. "But Rosalie isn't always invisible. Sometimes I can see her like a gray mist. Sometimes she whispers in my ear. Most of the time, it's too soft to make any sense out of it. But one time I said, 'Who's there?' and I heard 'Rosalie' repeated over and over. Since then she's told me lots."

"Well, *I* think you've got too much imagination for your own good," said Suellen with a laugh. She reopened her book.

"Don't believe me, then," said Maryjo angrily. She left the room. Suellen heard her stomping up the stairs to her bedroom, where she slammed the door.

A little later, Lady began to whimper in her sleep, as she sometimes did when having a doggie dream or nightmare. Then she suddenly woke up and sprang alert, growling. Suellen was so startled, she sat up suddenly, letting her book slip to the floor with a *thump*. "Easy, girl," she said, kneeling beside the dog, petting her head, trying to soothe her. But the dog just kept growling, with her eyes fixed on the stairs, visible through the living room archway.

"Stay," she ordered the dog, though it was clear that Lady had no intention of following. Going to the foot of the stairs, she called, "Maryjo! You okay?"

There was no response.

Quickly she ran up to the hallway above, her sneakers making little sound on the carpet. Maryjo's door was closed. From inside the room, Suellen could hear her sister's voice,

62

as though she were talking to someone. Occasionally she'd laugh, as if someone had told a joke. She must be on her cell phone, Suellen decided. Then she stopped. She was sure she could hear another, much softer voice—the person Maryjo was talking to. Her sister must have the volume way up on the phone if she could hear it through the door.

Suddenly there was silence, as if Maryjo had sensed her sister and was listening to make sure. "Are you out there, Suellen?" she yelled.

"Yes. I just wanted to be sure you were okay. Lady's doing that weird growling thing."

Her sister yanked the door open. "Rosalie was here," she said. Suellen couldn't help peering inside, half-expecting to see a swirl of fading gray mist. But there was nothing. Maryjo's phone was in the charger on the dresser, looking unused.

"Where did Rosalie go?" she challenged.

Maryjo shrugged. "Away. She won't tell me anything about it."

"You talk to her now?"

"Yeah. I see her more clearly, too. She's a little blond girl, about eight, with a hair ribbon and one of those fluffy skirts girls used to wear before we had jeans and stuff. And shiny black shoes—I forget the name."

"Mary Janes," said Suellen, who read a lot and remembered odd facts.

"Uh-huh. Anyhow, she just likes to come and talk. Sometimes she wants to play games like hide-and-seek or tag—kid stuff. She's always saying how lonely she is when she goes away."

"I think you should tell Mom and Dad about her."

"They won't believe me. And don't you go telling them my business," she added. "Swear by the double-X!" This had been their secret code since they were old enough to talk. Neither twin would break a double-Xed promise. With a sigh, Suellen agreed.

From this point on, Maryjo became more secretive. The door to her room was often closed. Suellen was sure she heard two voices sometimes through the door. At such times, Lady would growl, no matter where in the house she was. The dog, who used to roam freely upstairs and down, never went to the second floor anymore. In fact, she would often scratch and whine to be let out the back door when Maryjo was closeted in her room. The animal seemed uneasy when Maryjo was around and hovered around Suellen or their parents.

Suellen wanted to talk to her mother and father, but the power of the Double-X vow kept her silent.

She felt shut off from her twin, something that was especially painful for someone who had always shared everything—hopes and fears and dreams and birthdays—with the other.

Their parents sensed the changes and often asked Suellen about things, because Maryjo had grown increasingly argumentative and unwilling to talk. But Suellen gave vague answers, all the time growing increasingly worried about her sister.

Rosalie

There were still occasional incidents of objects being hurled across a room or of bathroom taps or lights turning on and off on their own. But they seemed to occur less often, even as Maryjo grew more distant. Suellen had the disturbing idea that all the energy Dr. Morris had called RSPK and that Maryjo called Rosalie was gathering around her sister. She felt helpless, yet knew that she ought to do *something*.

On Saturdays, Suellen earned some extra money helping old Mrs. Norman, a neighbor, with laundry and gardening and shopping. One day, helping to unpack groceries, she asked the woman, "You've lived here a long time, haven't you?"

"More than forty years," the other said. "My husband and I bought this place when we were first married. The children were born here. I expect I'll die here—though I don't plan on *that* too soon!" she added with a laugh.

"Do you remember the people who lived in our house before we moved here?" asked Suellen.

"I think so. Let me see. The Sorrentinos were there for almost fifteen years. Before them there was a family for just a year. Before that, it was the—let me think now—the Gilfillans. That was a sad story. They had a little girl, but she died suddenly. They stayed on, the two of them, rattling around in that big house. I knew Jean Gilfillan pretty well. Poor thing! She refused to leave, even after Hank passed away. She said she was sure the spirit of her little girl was around, and she couldn't leave her alone. Now what was the child's name . . . ?"

Double-Dare to Be Scared

"Rosalie," guessed Suellen, who had just put a pint of vanilla ice cream in the old woman's freezer.

"Yes. *Rosalie.* How did you know that?"

"I heard it somewhere, I guess," said Suellen, trying to sound offhand. "Do you remember her? The little girl?"

"Oh, yes!" the woman answered with feeling. "I don't want to speak ill of the dead, but she was a pistol, that one! Trouble from the get-go." She dropped her voice, as though someone might be listening. "I always wondered if there was something not quite right about her. She'd torment the neighborhood pets—until she got bitten or scratched. Then she'd go crying to her folks that the animal was to blame. I can't tell you how many fights began over her stories—her parents threatening one neighbor after another. A couple of pets had to be destroyed or given away. There were a lot of smaller children who seemed to get hurt when she was around. There was even a fire in the Murphys' garage that most people thought she had started, because the Murphys' son, the sweetest little boy you could imagine, told his parents that Rosalie had been forcing him to give her his lunch money every day. She got in plenty of trouble for that, even though her parents tried to claim the boy was a liar. She was what they used to call a 'bad seed.'"

"How did she die?"

"She caught a fever of some kind. One day she walked into the house, said she was feeling weak, and collapsed in front of her mother—poor woman, no matter that she'd defended the girl when the child clearly needed discipline.

66

Rosalie

Rosalie lingered about a week, but none of the doctors could say what was wrong with her. Jean and Hank wouldn't let her go to the hospital; they had round-the-clock nurses at the house. But none of it did any good. The child passed over, and her mother was never right after that. She kept insisting Rosalie was still in the house, somehow." Mrs. Norman suddenly shook her head, as though freeing herself of unwanted memories. "Let's have some cookies and tea before you have to go home," she said to Suellen.

"That would be nice," said the girl politely, though her head was filled to bursting with all that she had learned.

"The real Rosalie wasn't very nice," said Suellen to her sister that evening. They were sitting on opposite sides of Maryjo's bed.

"How do you know?" Maryjo demanded.

"Mrs. Norman remembers her. She knew the family. Rosalie hurt kids and dogs and cats. They thought she tried to burn down someone's garage when she got mad."

Maryjo made a sound between a laugh and a cough. "Old lady Norman probably can't remember her phone number. She's making up stories. Rosalie is a little girl who just needs a friend and wants to play."

"But she told me—"

"I don't care what she said!" cried Maryjo. "She's a liar, and you are, too, if you keep spreading her lies! Get out! I don't want to talk anymore."

She flopped down on the bed and turned her back to her sister. Suellen decided the best idea was to leave.

* * *

That night, Maryjo said she didn't feel well and refused to come down to dinner. A vase of silk flowers on the piano exploded to dust, scattering silk blooms all over the living room. Ellen Jarvie said to her husband, "That's it! We've got to sell this house." This was the start of the worst argument between her parents that Suellen had ever witnessed. Then Lady just went crazy: barking and growling at unseen things, before howling frantically and scrabbling at the back door until Suellen let her out. The cocker spaniel launched herself into the night like a creature with fifty devils after her. Because Maryjo's door was locked, Suellen (who would have liked to weather the parental storm in her sister's company) retreated to her own room to block out the sounds of arguing with the loudest CDs in her collection.

Because she fell asleep with her earphones on, Suellen wasn't sure when the arguing stopped and her parents went to bed. It wasn't until the morning, when she and her parents sat quietly at a tense breakfast that they noticed Lady was missing. "I let her out last night," Suellen admitted. "But I fell asleep before I let her back in."

"She's probably under the back porch," said her father. "Bring her in and give her food and fresh water." He sounded tired and angry; Suellen was quick to go look for Lady.

She searched and whistled for ten minutes before she found the dog, collapsed in the farthest corner of the yard. She sensed right away that Lady was dead. Unwilling to touch her, she ran for her mother and father. Her father was also sure she was dead, but he threw on jeans, wrapped the dog in an old blanket, and drove to the vet's. He returned two hours later without Lady. "She's gone," he said. "The vet said it was her heart—even though she wasn't an old dog and hadn't had any problems like this as far as he knew. Anyhow, he's going to . . . take care of her."

Maryjo stayed in bed during all of this. When Suellen tapped on her door, her sister got out of bed long enough to unlock the door, then buried herself under the covers again, as though she were freezing. When she learned that Lady was gone, she just shifted the covers in what Suellen guessed was a shrug. "Don't you care?" asked Suellen, surprised.

"No. She didn't like Rosalie, and Rosalie didn't like her."

Before Suellen could say anything, her mother came into the room. She ran her hand over Maryjo's forehead. "Honey, you're burning up. I'm calling the doctor right now."

The doctor decided Maryjo had a virus—nothing to worry about. Concern for Maryjo had cooled her parents' anger, Suellen was relived to see. But she couldn't get it out of her mind that her sister's illness, Lady's death, and Rosalie—whatever *she* might be—were somehow all connected. She was afraid for Maryjo.

That night, Suellen was awakened by the sound of soft footsteps moving down the hallway and padding down the stairs. The digital clock beside her bed showed 3:23 A.M. Pulling on her robe and slippers, she followed the sound to the head of the stairs. Looking down into the darkened hall, she was sure she saw her sister, wearing only her night-gown, step off the bottom stair and hurry toward the kitchen. Curious, Suellen followed. Hidden in the shadows, she saw the door across the hall from the kitchen, the one that led down to the garage, being drawn quietly shut. Was her sister sleepwalking? she wondered. Maybe it was the fever doing this. She followed the stairs to the landing, where the steps turned and continued at a right angle down to the garage floor. Feeling fearful, she peered around the corner. To her surprise, she saw Maryjo running back and forth, giggling, like someone playing tag with an imaginary friend. Her sister was barefoot on the chill concrete of the garage floor. Even in her warm robe, Suellen felt frozen. Yet Maryjo didn't seem to notice as she ran around, laughing like a very young child, her arms outstretched.

"Tag! You're it!" Maryjo suddenly cried. Then she began to bob and weave like someone avoiding being tagged. She was laughing with excitement, as she spun and danced away from an unseen touch. Her eyes were open, but they had a strangeness to them that made Suellen feel even colder than the chill air.

Maryjo's actions became even more frenzied; her laugh was so shrill, Suellen was surprised her parents hadn't wakened and come to investigate. It was all too crazy; Maryjo was going to make herself sicker. Not knowing what to do, Suellen cried, "Maryjo! Wake up!"

Startled, her sister stopped in midstep. She looked around, searching for the one who had cried out. She looked confused, as though she didn't know where she was. At the same moment, Suellen was sure she heard a childish voice, high and shrill, yell, "*Tag!* You're it."

Maryjo cried out and clutched her arm. "That's *freezing!*" Suddenly she began to tremble. Her two arms dropped to her sides like a pair of dead weights. Her legs began to shake. Screaming for her parents, Suellen ran and caught her twin as she collapsed. Maryjo's weight brought them both to their knees. "I feel so funny," her sister said, "like I'm a balloon filled with cold air. I can't feel my hands or feet!" she said. "I can't feel anything."

There were shouts from the head of the stairs.

"Down here!" Suellen screamed. "*Hurry!*" She hugged her sister, shocked at how cold the other girl's skin felt through the thin nightgown.

Maryjo never returned from the hospital. Two nights later, she died in the intensive care ward. The doctors talked about rare viruses and heart problems and so forth. Her parents felt they'd never truly know what caused Maryjo's death.

But Suellen guessed: it was Rosalie, who wanted a playmate with her wherever it was that ghosts spent time.

Suellen felt their home was empty without Maryjo and Lady. Her parents offered to buy her a new dog, but she just shrugged. She said nothing about Rosalie—certain that no one would believe her or believe that she had heard the girl's voice in the garage.

For a time, the family seemed to be making peace with all that had happened. But it was a chilly acceptance: the three of them sometimes moved through the house like three ghosts who had accidentally decided to haunt the same place.

And then one night while Suellen was reading in her room, the stuffed green frog that Maryjo had given her two birthdays ago suddenly floated off her bookshelf, drifted across the room, and landed gently in the middle of her open book. Something brushed the hair above her ear, tickling her. She was sure she heard faint laughter. She stood up, set her book on the seat of her chair, but kept hugging the frog.

"Maryjo?" she said. "Is that you?"

More giggles, as if two people were laughing. One laugh was childish, piping; the other sounded childlike, but older.

Suellen looked around the room but saw nothing. Yet, listening carefully, she could hear a faint *taptaptap* at her closed bedroom door. Afraid to open it, and afraid not to, she finally let her curiosity get the better of her.

At first she thought she was looking into a huge spider web of gray silk. Then she realized it was a gray mist filling the doorway—hazy enough so that she could see across the hall, could make out the details of the painting there.

Then the mist began to thicken into two figures, one taller than the other. In a moment, Suellen recognized her twin grinning at her, with her hands on the shoulders of the little blond girl in front of her.

"Maryjo," said Suellen, wondering whether she was having a dream. Maybe she had fallen asleep over her book.

Rosalie

"Your turn," said Maryjo, giving the younger girl's shoulders an affectionate squeeze.

"*Tag! You're it!*" cried Rosalie, gently touching the bare skin of Suellen's forearm. Instantly, Suellen felt freezing cold fill her, as though the blood in her veins were turning to ice.

Mountain Childers

Daniel Freed was on summer vacation at Anderson's Rest in the mountains of Kentucky with his parents and younger sisters. But he was bored—until he made friends with the Darraghs, an old couple living in a cabin not far from the pretty little lakeside resort.

Ruth Darragh was a great storyteller, recounting funny or frightening tales of the mountains. She always wore a brooch, an oval of carved whalebone that her husband, Joe, had given her. It had belonged to Joe's grandmother, who had been given it by his grandfather. This family treasure was her single piece of jewelry. "I'll wear it till the day I die," she said. It sparked many stories of the adventures of Joe's whaling grandfather.

Mountain Childers

Joe Darragh took Daniel fishing and introduced him to the art of whittling, and to the serious business of checkers. As the summer went on, Daniel spent more and more time with the couple. They never seemed old to him.

One day, Daniel was waiting impatiently for Joe to find his misplaced fishing creel, when he heard Ruth sing a snatch of song as she prepared apple pies in the kitchen. The woman didn't notice he was listening as she sang:

> I met Dom Darragh, who walked the land
> Wi' a mountain childer on either hand.
> They were lean an' long an' big in the eyes
> An' terrible hungry for their size.
>
> "Would they eat," said I, "if I'd give 'em food?"
> An' Dom, he whispered, "Indeed they would.
> "But they have no hunger for milk or bread—
> "They'd eat the two of us, heel an' head."

"Weird," said Daniel.

"Who's that?" asked Ruth, startled to find the boy standing there. For a moment, Daniel thought she looked almost afraid of him—or of something else. "Oh, Daniel—you give me a real turn."

"What's that song you were singing? Something about 'mountain childers.' What's that?"

"It's a bit o' foolishness my granny taught me," Ruth said quickly. "The 'childers' is just 'children.' There was old stories 'bout strange folks livin' way, way back in the hills, long ago. No one hardly ever saw them—and lucky if you didn't."

"Who was Dom Darragh? He has the same name as you."

"Mebbe a long-ago cousin or somethin'," answered Ruth, clearly unhappy to be talking about this. "My granny prob'ly made up the name. I only remember bits o' the song."

"Where did Dom find the children?" asked Daniel, eager to learn more despite the woman's unease.

"They found him."

"What happened to him?"

Seeming to sense he wouldn't let the matter drop, she answered him by singing:

An' down the road they went, the three,
While the ghost o' a laugh came back to me.
And poor Dom Darragh was nevermore seen,
Wi' the mountain childers an' him between.

"Creepy! Can you tell me more about the childers?"

"No! And don't go talkin' 'bout such things! It's bad luck." She glanced up and said quickly, "Here's Joe standin' outside waitin' for you. Go fishin', and don't go tellin' your folks I've been fillin' your head with nonsense!"

As they sat beside the creek, Daniel tried to get more information from Joe about the mountain childers. But the old man grew uncomfortable with the boy's questions and put an end to the matter by declaring, "Rubbish! Old woman shouldn't be dredgin' up such codswallop." Daniel was going to push further, but the old man seemed upset, so he decided not to spoil a day that had already brought the two of them good fishing, three trout in the creel, and hours of sunlight left.

Still, Daniel couldn't let things go. He continued to probe

the mystery of the strange hill-country folk. But when he asked the old-timers who lived in and around Anderson's Rest, they were reluctant to discuss the matter. Most dismissed the childers as "fairy tales," but there was unease in some eyes, which Daniel was sharp enough to recognize as a sign that not everyone believed that the accounts were only made-up stories.

Soon after this, the boy stopped by the Darraghs' cabin to show Joe how his carving of a hawk was coming along. Joe wasn't there, but Ruth was. And she looked worried. She sat him down by the kitchen table and put a plate of fresh-baked oatmeal cookies—his favorite—on the oilcloth that served as tablecloth. Then she sat down across from him and bit her lower lip, as though she needed to say something but didn't know where to begin. At last, she took a deep breath and said, "I hear talk you been askin' 'round 'bout the 'childers.'"

"Yeah. But no one will tell me much of anything." He shrugged. "A few told me to stop asking questions."

"Well, now, that's some good advice."

"They're only stories. *You* said that's all they were."

She sighed. "They is. But the world's a funny place, and these mountains is a funnier place than most. There's things as happen here don't happen anywheres else. You may not b'lieve somethin', but you don't want t' provoke somethin', neither."

"Either something is real or it isn't," said Daniel, with a ten-year-old's stubbornness.

"Sometimes talkin' too much can make you b'lieve," said Ruth.

"Like when we play 'Mary Worth.'"

Ruth shook her head, not understanding.

"It's a ghost story—well, a game really. There was supposed to be this woman named Mary Worth. One day there was a car accident, and her face got all torn up, and she died. But people say her ghost hangs around. If you stand in front of a mirror in the dark and say three times, 'I believe in you, Mary Worth,' she'll appear in the mirror. Then you have to turn on the light and run away fast, or she'll reach out and try to scratch off your face."

Ruth made a face. "You play *that?*"

"Once," Daniel admitted. "Nothing happened. But another time a friend did it, and he swears the ghost leaned out of the mirror and clawed him before he got the light on. He had a big scratch down the side of his face. Everybody said he'd scratched himself climbing a tree and made up the story. But he always said it was real."

"Playin' wi' fire," said Ruth. "There's things as should be left alone. Your ghost is one; childers is another. Now, not another word." She cut the boy off before he could protest.

He sat and ate more cookies in silence, while she bustled around the kitchen, until Joe returned.

*D*aniel was surprised, several days later, when he went to visit the old couple and found they had company. He'd gone around to the back of the cabin to ask Joe to go lake-fishing for wide mouthed bass. Tying up some bean vines in the garden, Joe said, "These is some grandcousins of our'n. They's from Arkhamville, way back in the hills."

The boy and girl sat on the top step of the porch. The boy wore bib overalls; the girl, an old-fashioned dress that reached to her ankles (it looked like a hand-me-down that had passed through many hands). The boy was blond and had a large head and rough-hewn features; the girl was dark-haired, with pigtails tied with frayed bits of red ribbon. They looked enough alike that it was easy to see they were brother and sister. Both were barefoot and skinny, and they didn't smile. They stared at Daniel with wide, unwelcoming eyes.

"Hi," said Daniel.

The girl looked at her brother. He muttered something that Daniel couldn't understand. Part of the problem was that the boy barely opened his mouth when he spoke. Were they shy? Daniel wondered. Or ashamed of their teeth? He knew that many of the poorer folk in the area couldn't afford a dentist (this had come up in a discussion with his parents some weeks before) and tried to hide crooked or missing teeth this way.

Ruth Darragh brought out tall glasses of lemonade for the children, who accepted them without thanks. "Always thirsty, these two," she murmured. She offered Daniel a glass only as an afterthought. She seemed distracted and uncomfortable to have Daniel around. And Joe kept glancing up anxiously from his work. All the time Daniel sat on the lower step sipping lemonade, he was aware of the adults constantly watching him and the two cousins. Even when Ruth went back into the kitchen, he saw her lingering, peering through the screen door.

Daniel began to feel jealous, seeing how much attention the older Darraghs gave the newcomers. Their cabin had always been his special place to visit. He tried to keep the resentment out of his voice when he asked, "How long are you guys gonna stay?"

The boy shrugged. The girl just looked at him over the rim of her glass.

"What grade are you in at school?" he asked, glancing from one to the other.

The boy shrugged again.

This time the girl answered. Like her brother, she kept her mouth mostly closed, but she was easier to understand. "We learn t'home."

When he asked them their names, a look passed between the two. Then the boy said, "You kin call me Jack."

"Addie," said the girl.

At that moment, Ruth came out on the porch with a platter of cold fried chicken, which she set between the young cousins. They grabbed up the meat, chewing noisily; but they kept their heads turned and hands angled so that Daniel couldn't see their poor teeth. It was clear to him that the greedykins weren't about to share anything. "Always hungry, these two," said Ruth, glancing over at Daniel. "Growin' children." Then she added, "I've got extra chicken inside, if you'd like."

Though he really was hungry, Daniel shook his head. "That's okay. I had a big breakfast. And I really have to be going, since you've got company and all."

Ruth looked down at Addie and Jack. The boy was chewing on a chicken wing. Daniel could hear the bones crunch, so he realized the boy must have some solid teeth. Addie was sucking noisily on a leg bone and running her finger across the platter to skim up any grease that was left. *They must not get nearly enough to eat back home,* Daniel thought.

"That all?" asked Jack, spitting bone splinters onto the plate.

"I could fix biscuits an' honey," says Ruth.

The boy nodded.

"With *lots* o' honey," added Addie, wiping her mouth with the back of her hand, then licking it so as not to miss the tiniest fleck of grease.

Ruth reached down a hand to pick up the platter with its litter of bones. She hesitated a moment, her eyes flicking left-right, girl-boy, in an anxious way that made Daniel think of someone considering removing a dish from in front of a strange dog, afraid of getting bitten if the animal wasn't through eating. He saw the woman's mouth tighten, then lift the plate with a trembling hand.

"We're still *hungry,*" Jack said sullenly.

"*Hungry,*" his sister echoed.

"I'll get biscuits and so forth direc'ly," said Ruth, retreating into the kitchen. The screen door slammed behind her.

Suddenly, Daniel wanted to be away from the place and these two *totally weird* kids. He stood up from the lower step, brushed off the seat of his pants, set his empty lemonade glass on the next step up, and said good-bye to the children. But they had their backs to him. They were watching the screen door, drawn to the sounds of Ruth preparing fresh food, with the intentness of a retriever spotting a duck or a cat watching a mousehole.

"Goin'?" asked Joe. The old man was giving all his attention to the bean stakes.

"Yeah, I guess," Daniel replied. "I was gonna ask you about fishing for bass, but looks like you might be too busy."

"With . . . *kin* . . . visitin'—well, y'know how family is," said Joe, sounding uncomfortable. He jerked a knot too tight, and part of the vine suddenly snapped off.

"Maybe we can go fishing when they're gone," Daniel said quickly.

"That'd be real nice," said Joe, standing up and stretching his back after bending over the vines. The bones in his back made an audible *crack*. The children turned suddenly to look at Joe and Daniel. They grinned. There was something so unpleasant about their smiles that Daniel felt chilled in the warm afternoon sun. "Tell Ruth I said good-bye," he told Joe.

It took all his nerve to walk away from the cabin and not break into a panicked run. The urge to escape did not leave him until he had turned a bend in the path, and the cabin was hidden from view by a stand of dusty pines.

"You're back early," his mother said, looking up from the book she was reading.

"Joe and Ruth have company. Relatives."

"Who's visiting?"

But Daniel didn't want to discuss the strange mountain cousins; he just shrugged. "Where's Dad?" he asked, to change the subject.

"He took Amy and Beth for a walk and to get Popsicles at the bait shop."

"I think I'll see if I can find them," he said, hurrying toward the pier area. The idea of something so familiar after the strangeness of the past hour seemed a relief.

From that afternoon, Daniel pretty much lost touch with the Darraghs. Once or twice, he went to the cabin. But he always stopped short of talking to anyone. From the shade of the surrounding trees, he sometimes glimpsed Joe or Ruth doing chores. But their young cousins were always sitting or standing side by side, watching the adults like guard dogs. He didn't dare approach any closer. He hated the kids for the way they seemed to have taken over his friends' household and lives.

The last time he saw Joe, the old man was walking back up the hot, dusty road from Meckel's Grocery, holding two big brown shopping bags. In the time since Daniel had seen him, the old man had grown shockingly thin—whittled down to little more than skin and bones. When Daniel stopped to say hello, the other's arms trembled so he nearly dropped one of the bags. The boy was sure he saw some terrible fear in the man's eyes.

"Can I help?" asked Daniel, reaching to take one of the bags.

"*NO!*" shouted Joe, pulling back, clutching the bags like sacks of gold. Then his tone softened, "I'm fine. Don't need no help."

He didn't look fine.

Daniel said, "Is something wrong? Can I help?"

"Ruth's got a fever."

"Did you call—"

"She's bein' took care of," said Joe. He shifted the grocery bags and started along the road.

"Please let me help," begged Daniel.

"You can't come 'round," said Joe. "Might ketch th' fever. *Stay away.*" He said the last two words with such force that Daniel backed off, as the old man trudged up the path without once looking back.

The Freed family's vacation ended on Labor Day weekend. Though he hadn't seen either of the Darraghs since his tense meeting with Joe, on the day before they were to leave, Daniel was determined to say good-bye to his friends. He also wanted to be sure that they were all right.

But their cabin was deserted. He knocked on the front door, then went around to the back. Through the locked screen door, he could see into the kitchen. A chair had been knocked over; the table had been shoved against the wall; a strip of the oilcloth cover hung down, as though ripped free. Peering further into the shadows, he saw flour and sugar scattered on the floor from overturned canisters on the counter.

He cupped his hands around his mouth and called, "Joe! Ruth!" But there was no answer. Just when he was thinking of punching open the screen door and letting himself into the silence, he heard laughter behind him.

Startled, he turned and saw Jack and Addie, who had

come around the corner of the house. Now looking well-fed and healthy, they grinned up at him. At the collar of the girl's worn dress was an oval of white, shining in the sun. From the distance and the sun's glare, Daniel couldn't be certain, but he thought it was Ruth's whalebone cameo.

"Whatchu want, boy?" the girl's brother asked suspiciously.

"To say good-bye to Joe and Ruth."

"Ain't here," said the girl. She took a step closer, smiling at him, closemouthed and sinister. "You hadn't oughtta be, neither."

Now Daniel could clearly see that the white oval at her throat was Ruth's brooch.

His anger momentarily overcoming his fear, he stomped down the back steps to face the strange twosome. "That belongs to Ruth!" he said, pointing at the bit of carved whalebone.

"She give it t'me," Addie said carelessly. "Said she don't need it no more."

"It b'longs t' sister now," said Jack, standing behind the girl and putting his hands protectively on her shoulders. The sickening grin stayed in place, but his eyes were dark and threatening now. "Git you gone, boy, if'n you know what's good f'you."

He spoke softly, but Daniel could hear clearly the threat behind the words.

Daniel suddenly had two recollections of Ruth in her kitchen. In the first, she was showing him the brooch pinned to her dress, saying, *"I'll wear it till the day I die."*

86

The second memory was of her rolling piecrust while she sang,

> *"Would they eat," said I, "if I'd give 'em food?"*
> *An' Dom, he whispered, "Indeed they would.*
> *"But they have no hunger for milk or bread—*
> *"They'd eat the two of us, heel an' head."*

Suddenly terrified, Daniel ran for his folks' cabin. He heard the chilling laughter of the other children in his imagination, long after he was out of earshot. After his parents had calmed him down enough, he insisted that his father call the police. Because he was so worked up, his father did call the sheriff.

That evening, the sheriff reported that he had found nothing amiss at the Darraghs' cabin. It was locked. Through the windows, he could see that the floor was swept, the beds were made, everything seemed in order. "Seems like those folks went off—maybe to visit kin back in the hills." He made it clear that he was not interested in pursuing matters. Mr. Freed apologized for the trouble to which they'd put the man. Daniel's mother did her best to assure her son that his friends were fine.

But Daniel spent a fretful night listening to sounds outside the window. He heard, he was sure, faint laughter tangled in the night breezes that blew down from the mountains.

As the family drove away the next morning, he was certain he saw Jack and Addie watching the family's SUV from the shadow of a cluster of pines, where the road turned sharply. But before he could point them out to anyone else, they'd slipped behind the trees out of sight.

Double-Dare to Be Scared

*   *   *

On the day school began the following week, Daniel's mother told him as he finished breakfast, "Some classmates of yours are here to walk you to school."

Puzzled, the boy stepped out onto the front porch. Jack and Addie were waiting for him, hand in hand. They had grown thinner since he'd seen them last. Both were grinning, but there was no laughter in their staring eyes in their big heads. He wanted to run back into the house, but his legs were frozen; he tried to call for his mother, but the words caught in his throat.

First the girl, then her brother, extended a hand. "C'mon, boy!" they urged. Like the prisoner of a dream, Daniel put his right hand into Jack's and his left hand into Addie's. Step by resisting step, he followed them to the sidewalk, where they turned and began walking south.

"My school is the other way," Daniel protested, his voice dry as dust.

"You're playin' hooky today," said the girl. Her brother added, "You don't have t'worry about school ever agin."

Somewhere behind him, Daniel heard his mother calling after him, "Daniel, you forgot your books and homework!"

He wanted to answer her, but all he could do was sing softly, as his eyes filled with tears,

> An' down the road they went, the three,
> While the ghost o' a laugh came back to me.
> An' poor Dan Freed was nevermore seen,
> Wi' the mountain childers an' him between.

Class Cootie

Anthony was slow to understand a lot of things: multiplication tables and prepositions and how to spell *principal*. But he knew that everyone at Charlotte Forten Elementary School—the teachers, the staff, and the 823 students—thought him a fool and laughed at him. Sometimes, like his classmates, they snorted loudly behind their hands when he answered wrongly in class; sometimes he sensed that his teachers dissed him politely, because they thought he'd never learn.

He'd even heard some teachers tell "Anthony stories" in the lounge or after school, when they thought the halls and the classrooms were empty, or while walking to their parked cars. But Anthony heard. Or other students heard and turned the stories into jokes during recess. There were stories of first-grade Anthony breaking into tears because the visiting *author* of popular picture books wasn't *Arthur* the anteater, come round for a personal visit at school. Second-grade Anthony telling the mayor, who had come for a social studies visit, that he had bad breath. Third-grade Anthony fighting with classmates who insisted on telling him that Santa Claus, the Easter bunny, and the tooth fairy were made-up stories.

School was never a happy place for Anthony. He knew he looked as awkward as the way he spoke. In his eyes, his classmates were all good-looking, while he saw himself as ugly shapes thrown together: a salad with a misshapen bell pepper of a head on top of an eggplant body—thin-shouldered and big-butted—with spindly, celery-stalk arms and legs that ended in hands and feet that were as thick and awkward as bunches of carrots.

His full and proper name was Anthony Edward Kovacovich. But it was everywhere written "Anthony E. Kovacovich." Now the "E" had come to stand for "Earwax," after one of the students in his third-grade class had spotted a dribble of yellow wax escaping from his ear when he'd had an infection and refused to tell the school nurse, no matter the pain he had felt.

Anthony lived with his grandmother, Nana Olga. She had come from somewhere in Eastern Europe with her son and his wife, Anthony's mother, before Anthony was born. But Anthony's father had fallen in with what his mother had called "bad fellows," had had some minor run-ins with the law, and had finally drifted off shortly after his child was born. Anthony's mother had followed soon after. So there was just Nana Olga and Anthony. Neither one had heard from the boy's parents in more than a year. In his heart, Anthony was sure that their disappointment with him—their ugly, stupid child—had driven them away. But Nana Olga loved him deeply, and that made up for almost everything else the world had not given him or others had done to him.

The other kids called his grandmother a "witchy woman." They made fun of her large, brightly printed dresses, her long white hair reaching to her waist, and the big earrings and gaudy necklaces she wore. She made poultices and brewed herb teas when Anthony was sick. But Nana Olga couldn't protect him at school. True, she threatened from time to time to punish his classmates and teachers and anyone who hurt him using powers she claimed all the women in her family had inherited. But Anthony begged her not to use this magic, as he truly believed she could. His hope was that one day, like the sun breaking through after a rainstorm, people would begin to like him. And if Nana Olga worked her spells, he reasoned, it would make people like him even less than they did—which was not at all.

Even Mr. Marchand, his teacher, made fun of him in sly ways. Anthony sensed that something about his looks and his slow way of answering made the adults as well as the children at Charlotte Forten want to hurt him with words, when shoves and pinches and spitballs to the back of the head were out of the question.

He was called the "class cootie," after his "book buddy,"

ANTHONY
EARWAX
KOVACOVICH
COOTIUS MAXIMUS

a first-grader, had refused to share a desk with him, saying, "I don't want Anthony cooties on me." The child had been sent to the principal and had given Anthony a badly written apology, but the damage was done. Anthony was now officially third grade "class cootie" and, soon enough, "school cootie." Kids gave him a wide berth in the hallway; anyone who came within a few inches of him made exaggerated scratching motions.

Life, which had been bad enough, had suddenly become worse for him.

But the worst came on the day he went to school and found that someone—probably a fifth grader—had found an old Cootie game. Whoever it was had put the plastic bug, with its black body and six pink legs, so it dangled in the front of the trophy case at the entrance to the school. Twin green antennae stuck out of the blue head, while at the mouth curled a snaky tongue like a butterfly's feeding tube. The yellow button eyes seemed to watch Anthony thoughtfully as the boy read the hand-lettered sign proclaiming, "Anthony Earwax Kovacovich, Cootius Maximus." In prying open and resealing the lock, they'd broken the mechanism, so the display would stay where it was all through the day, until the janitor could clear it out after school.

Mr. Marchand, like all the teachers, made a show of disapproval. But Anthony could see the smile waiting to be set free in the teachers' lounge, the amusement in his eyes that would turn into chuckles in the parking lot. Anthony felt the whole school was laughing at him behind his back.

The weather that day, which had begun with heavy black clouds hanging over the town and distant Detroit, now turned to storm. Lightning flashed. The lights in the school dimmed several times but never actually went out. Someone started a rumor that Anthony's Nana Olga was causing the bad weather because they had made fun of her grandson. In the close confines of the school, belief took root: children began looking at Anthony in a fearful way. For a moment, this made him feel powerful: but he quickly dismissed such thoughts. He wanted people to like him— not to be *afraid* of him.

The day grew darker. The wind and rain grew fiercer. In the lunchroom, the storm made the already restless children more unruly. When Anthony sat down, there was much pushing and shoving to "get away from the cootie." Someone threw a glob of Jell-O, which hit him on the side of the face. It quickly erupted into a food fight, with most of the things thrown at Anthony. As the teachers went around collaring the worst troublemakers and threatening mass detentions, meanness turned to anger. "It's all Anthony's fault" became the tribal cry.

Unable to bear any more of the shouts and laughter and thrown food, the boy broke and ran for it. He wanted only home and the comfort of Nana Olga's healing hugs.

Many students who had already returned from lunch and were engaged in classroom activities (because the rain had canceled outdoor recess) watched from the windows as Anthony dodged between two parked cars and ran into the middle of Maple Avenue in front of the school. So there were countless young witnesses as a car—slamming on its brakes but sliding on the rain-slicked road—struck the boy. Anthony smashed into a parked car and died instantly.

The school held a memorial service for the boy in the cafetorium the following week. Teachers and a few parents sat on folding chairs; the students sat on the chilly linoleum and listened as the principal, then Mr. Marchand and several others, spoke about what an asset Anthony had been to the school. They said his passing was a loss for them all. To the children the words seemed to be about someone else. Anthony had been the "class cootie"; no one liked him; no one really mourned his death. His parents were not there. Even Mr. Marchand, who spoke so sadly about him, had often made fun of Anthony in class. Most of the children recognized dishonesty as they listened to the flowery speeches from the adults on stage, who talked about a boy they had never bothered to care about or get to know.

Then Nana Olga, who was sitting quietly off to one side, wearing a black dress of some shiny material and an uncharacteristically small black hat with black roses on it, was asked to speak to the assembly.

She walked slowly to the podium, pulled the microphone down to her mouth (since the previous speaker, Mr. Marchand, was at least a head taller than she), and said, "So many kind words for my sweet Anthony. But where were your kind words before this? I don't recall my little boy coming home ever to tell me what nice things you people said to him. I *do* recall him coming home in tears many times. I do recall coaxing from him the unkind things you . . ." Here Nana Olga pointed at the assembled children, most of whom shook their heads in denial, though some turned red and looked away from the woman's fierce gaze. ". . . and you . . ." Here she pointed at the staff and teachers seated behind her, who squirmed uncomfortably in their seats. ". . . said about him plenty of times. You hounded him to death," she said, nodding her head. "Oh, yes, you most certainly did. Well, save your polite words; they're too late . . . to help Anthony or to help yourselves."

As if to underline her last words, the rainstorm that had been threatening all morning broke loose with a tremendous thunderclap. Many of the kids yelped in fright. They cringed as Nana Olga marched straight down the aisle between the seated ranks. The woman never looked right or left, never once looked back at the stage, where the adults watched her depart as they whispered to one another.

Rain pounded against the hall's high windows. The principal took the podium and, after clearing his throat several times, said, "I'm afraid Anthony's grandmother was very upset. Clearly, she misses Anthony terribly. But time will heal her and all of us. Now, look to your teachers to begin returning to your classrooms. And there will be no outdoor recess today, due to the rain."

Mr. Marchand was in the middle of history class when the lights flickered and died overhead, following a particularly loud roll of thunder and an eye-blinding burst of lighting. The principal was in the middle of a phone conversation with a member of the school board when the lights failed and the phone gave such an earsplitting burst of static that he dropped the earpiece on his desk with a *thump.* When it was clear that the line was dead, he picked up his cell phone to redial the school board office. But, strangely enough, his cell phone was dead, too. In the outer office, his secretary was sitting in front of her extinguished computer screen, making sure that the console was fully shut down to prevent damage from a surge when the power went back on.

"May I borrow your cell phone?" the principal asked.

She dutifully fished her personal phone out of her purse. To her dismay, she found that her phone was dead, too.

"Well," said her boss, "we seem to be temporarily cut off from the world."

Further conversation was cut off by shouts from the fourth- and fifth-grade classrooms down the hall. These were the classrooms that faced onto Maple Avenue. These were the children who had witnessed Anthony's fatal accident.

"What now?" asked the principal with a sigh. "What else could possibly go wrong?"

He went into room 4-C. The children were crowding against the windows. Even the teacher and her aide were pointing to something outside.

"What on earth . . . ?" the man asked, adjusting his glasses. Then he saw.

The sky was raining insects—massive, brightly colored bugs with black, yellow, green, and red bodies. When they hit the ground, they scuttled forward on pink legs. Green antennae moved rapidly detecting sounds; glittering yellow eyes darted back and forth, seeking movement. These shiny, impossible creatures had glistening metal claws; and the ends of their eagerly unrolled feeding tubes, lashing back and forth, had wicked-looking tiny blades. Hordes of them poured across the parking lot and up the steps to the main entrance to the school. Already the first creatures had swarmed to window level, and were whipping blades and snapping claws at the children who were backing away as quickly as possible. Someone began to scream. Abruptly, there was screaming everywhere. The bugs were piling up against the window.

"Everyone get into the hall, *now*," ordered the principal, trying to regain some bit of control.

Then the first windowpane exloded inward from its frame, the shards of glass scattering across the floor. There was the din of gnawing, gnashing, clicking, buzzing everywhere, as the brightly colored creatures poured through the opening. But the sounds they made were quickly drowned out by the shouts and screams that filled both floors of the darkened school.

Half-past Midnight

If you travel west on the Massachusetts Turnpike, past Springfield and the Connecticut River, you'll come to the town of Ansell, on the edge of Ansell's Pond. It's a quaint village, tucked into the woods, with the slopes of the Berkshires in the background. The town's main attraction is the Treadwell Inn, which has stood for close to three centuries and attracts tourists who stay overnight or, at the very least, have a leisurely meal at the nearby Coach House Restaurant. Both the inn and the restaurant are supposed to be haunted, though no one can agree on how many ghosts might be involved or whose spirits they might be.

Even more eerie are the stories about Ansell's Pond. In colonial days, there were reports that on nights when the moon was full, witches would dance across the pond, their bare feet edged in white fire, their red skirts billowing in the night wind. All the while, shadowy figures would creep along the shore: pigs with the heads of cows, roosters with the heads of pigs, goat-footed rabbits, and wolves with the faces of women.

The younger children avoided the pond as soon as evening began to fall. But the older kids in town would often organize campouts on nights when the moon was full, hoping to catch sight of witches or other creatures that some people swore still haunted the pond.

These stories fascinated Lucille Giroux, a new sixth-grader at Larkin Middle School. She came from a small town, whose name none of the other kids could pronounce, in French Canada. She moved in with her aunt Henriette and uncle Alain Giroux, who lived in a small cottage on the outskirts of Ansell, not far from the pond. Though they had lived in the town for thirteen years, people knew very little about them. They were polite but kept mostly to themselves. They were the only relatives of the girl, whose mother had died when she was born and whose father had reportedly been killed in a hunting accident.

Lucille was pretty and had the ghost of an accent, which intrigued the sixth-grade boys, though the girls snubbed her, jealous of the attention she was getting. Samantha Cross disliked her the most. Though Sam had broken up with Nate Hendryx to date the class president (who was also captain of the football team), Sam found herself growing jealous of the interest her ex-boyfriend was showing in the new girl.

One day, while Sam was talking to several of her friends in the cafeteria, she spotted Lucille walking past. Changing the subject abruptly and raising her voice so that the other girl was sure to hear, Sam said, "I hear *she* believes in crazy stuff like ghosts and witches and *ludens.*"

"You mean cough drops?" another girl asked.

"No, silly," said Lucille, who knew they were making fun of her. "*Lutins.* They are like *les fées*—fairies—yes! They are very real. Also *les loups-garous*—werewolves. One should not make fun of these things."

"One zhould not make fun of zeese tings," Samantha mocked. Her friends laughed far more loudly than necessary.

Lucille shrugged, then added, "Those who make laugh at *lutins* and such may find themselves stolen by the fairies or wind up *le souper*—supper—for *un loup-garou.*" But her warning only made them laugh more loudly. Shaking her head, the girl continued on her way.

Things grew tenser when Sam and her group spotted Nate strolling home with Lucille. The two ambled along, not aware of the glares sent their way from a cyclone fence full of girls, clinging to the far side of the metal mesh like bats to a cave wall.

"A bunch of us are going down to the pond on Friday," Nate was saying. "It's a full moon, and we're doing a ghost-watch."

"What's that?" Lucille asked.

"We hang out on the shore, roast hot dogs, and cook s'mores. We watch to see if a witch or something else shows up."

"Such things are not games," said Lucille. "Still, it might be *intéressant* to see what might come to your party." Then she sighed. "But I do not think my aunt and uncle would let me go. I am never allowed to stay out beyond eleven o'clock—even on a weekend."

"Heck, most of us have to be home by ten," said Nate.

"Then I will ask," said Lucille, brightening.

She did come to Ansell's Pond on Friday night. Nate quickly left Sam and some other friends with mouths full of s'mores, beside a fire supervised by several older brothers and sisters, when Lucille strolled down the beach from the direction of the Giroux cottage.

"It's late," Nate said. "I didn't think you'd come."

"My relatives were not happy," she said with a smile. "But I told them everyone at school would mock me if I did not come. In the end, here I am. But I must be home before eleven."

They avoided the fireside, where Sam and the others were watching their every move. Nate found them seats on a fallen log some distance away from the clusters of kids and older siblings scattered along the pond's shore, watching for hints of ghosts or monsters. Lucille gazed eagerly across the moonlit water. After a while she complained, "I see nothing. I feel nothing."

"You won't," said Nate, "but it's fun to party. And I like being here with you." Then he turned away, as if she could see how red his face had become, even in the dark.

But Lucille didn't notice his embarrassment. "Look!" she said suddenly, pointing across the water. He looked, and there, halfway across the moon-silvered surface, he was sure he saw a double flicker of white fire supporting a shadowy, billowy figure. His mouth and throat went dry. Was he looking at a ghostly witch skimming the pond, which now looked like a floor of glass? He heard shouts from down the beach. Kids were yelling and pointing: they had seen something, too.

Then the brush behind him stirred. He whirled around to see . . . he wasn't sure. It looked like a girl's face on the body of a huge dog. But it vanished so quickly, he thought he might have imagined it. When he looked across the pond, the shadow with the fiery feet had also disappeared. The watchers on the shore were talking excitedly, drifting back to huddle around the fire.

Something rustled again in the bushes behind them. "Let's go back to where the others are," Nate said, suddenly standing up. He reached out his hand to Lucille. But when she started to get up, she suddenly cried, "Something has stung my cheek!" She touched her fingers to her face, and they came away bloody.

"It's not a bite," said Nate, drawing her into the circle of firelight. "Someone threw something."

They looked around but saw only Sam and her pals staring back at them, all innocence and pretended concern.

"I am sure I know who did this," said Lucille.

"I can guess," Nate said. He looked around for Sam, but she had moved away to another group.

"How bad is it?" asked Nate.

"Not as bad as someone else would hope," Lucille

answered, dabbing at the cut with a bit of Kleenex. "Still, I think it is late enough for me to be going home now." She started back up the shore and waved him off when he wanted to follow. "My guardians don't like visitors after dark."

The next day, Sam led a chorus of laughter when she asked Lucille, "What happened to your face? Cut yourself shaving?"

Lucille touched the small flesh-colored Band-Aid on her cheek. "It is nothing. A little sting from a careless insect." She stared at Samantha until the other looked away. Lucille smiled and continued on her way.

"Weird-o," Sam muttered.

Soon after this, the English teacher—who also directed the sixth-grade play each year—announced that she would be holding auditions for the musical *Cinderella*. Among the hopefuls were Lucille and Samantha. Lucille won easily when their teacher discovered that she had a beautiful singing voice. Samantha took the part of one of the ugly stepsisters with bad grace. The fact that Nate was chosen to play Prince Charming only added to her anger—and her determination to break up whatever was happening between Nate and the other girl. She was still dating the class president, but Lucille had become a challenge to her.

At first, Lucille's aunt and uncle refused to let her take the lead in the play. But then the teacher-director assured them that the evening performances over two weekends would never run later than ten o'clock. And Nate's mother promised to drive Lucille home after each performance, since neither older Giroux could drive. With these guarantees, the girl's guardians agreed to let her be in the play. They even came to the opening-night performance, applauded loudly, and called Lucille their *petite Cendrillon* — little Cinderella.

But Sam saw how anxiously Lucille watched the clock each evening after the play ended; she seemed to grow more and more nervous with each passing minute. "I wonder what happens if she stays out past midnight?" Sam asked one of her friends.

Someone said, "Maybe she turns into a pumpkin." Someone else said, "That creepy aunt and uncle of hers probably read her the riot act. They've been in town all these years, and they can't even speak English without making it sound French."

"They're all losers," Sam summed up. But an idea was taking shape. "Next Saturday is the cast party after the last performance. I know *Leew-seal* is going to stay awhile, because Nate told me. We could set the clocks back an hour and do the same with our own watches."

"Nate's mom always drives her home. She'll be keeping an eye on the time."

"Nate's Mom is a chatterbox," said Sam. "It's easy to get her talking about anything, then she just forgets what's going on. I'll talk to her. She won't be any problem at all."

That was the plan.

*   *   *

Double-Dare to Be Scared

When the applause died down after the last Saturday performance, Sam and her commandos went into action, setting all the clocks and watches they could find back an hour. There was a wall-mounted digital clock, but they blanked it out with a swatch of black electrical tape.

As the last-night audience filed out of the school auditorium, the cast, most still in costume, returned to the stage area to scarf down pizza slices, potato chips and peanuts and retrieve cans of soda from donated coolers. Sam took Mrs. Hendryx aside and started up a conversation that soon had the woman recalling trips to Spain and childhood memories. Time ceased to have meaning for her, as Sam intended. Lucille and Nate wandered off, paper plates heaped high, and sat by themselves. Around them were the painted flats representing the palace ballroom where Cinderella had met Prince Charming and later married him. Nate wasn't wearing a watch, since his had been broken when he'd attempted a 360 kick flip on his skateboard the week before and taken a bad spill.

Sam had Jenny Moore—a younger girl who wanted to join Sam's group—ask to borrow Lucille's gold watch, pretending to admire it, then setting it back an hour before she returned it.

People talked, laughed, shouted—no one seemed to notice that the time was off by an hour. A few people, whose watches hadn't been tampered with, glanced at them and left. But there were enough lingerers who seemed content to let the time be what it seemed to be. Lucille and Nate were among them. They talked about some of the funny

106

things that had happened at performances, about school-work, about their feelings for each other. Sam watched them with anger and satisfaction that the night would mean trouble for Lucille, if her efforts paid off.

The crowd had thinned. The clocks and watches showed 11 P.M. Mrs. Hendryx was telling a long, involved story about the family's cruise to Alaska to anyone who would listen.

Suddenly Lucille stood up, spilling a half-eaten pizza slice and a handful of potato chips onto the floor. She pressed her hands to her face. "I feel so strange," she told Nate, who was staring at her, his mouth full of pizza. *"What time is it?"*

"It's just after eleven. Look at your watch," he said.

She looked, then shook her head. "Something is wrong!" she cried. The talk and laughter amid the backstage setting died away, as people turned to stare at the girl. Sam nudged her friends. *Payback time,* she mouthed.

Mrs. Hendryx looked at her watch, then said, "Am I an hour off? It's *midnight,* according to my watch."

Lucille screamed. She began to spin around and around, as though she could no longer remember where she was or who she was. She continued to scream, even though several teachers and parents were grabbing at her, trying to calm her down. But she batted aside their hands and arms as she spun, the skirts of her Cinderella bridal gown making a circle of white around her.

Her face grew long, snoutlike; her blue eyes turned yellow; the dainty white gloves she had worn (loaned by

Nate's grandmother) shredded as claws burst through the antique lace. Snarling, the black dog or wolf or whatever it was bit and slashed away the remains of the costume. Panicked people, fleeing toward the exits, knocked over sets and kicked aside props as they ran. Mrs. Hendryx grabbed Nate and hugged him to her. The creature, its yellow eyes edged in red, stared at them, growling, then turned its attention to the others flying from the auditorium. With a howl, the monster landed on the gym teacher's back, sending him sprawling. *Snick-snap* the jaws opened, closed. . . . Then the beast raced on to another victim. And another.

Some people had reached the main entrance to the auditorium. Most hadn't gotten past the doors.

One who had was Samantha, still in her stepsister costume of green, with green-sequined shoes with silver bows on them. Behind her, one of her friends tripped and screeched for help, but Sam never looked back. She flew down the steps toward the parking lot.

But something caught her two-thirds of the way down, then fled into the dark woods that circled Larkin Middle School on three sides.

Arriving a short time later in response to frantic calls from survivors' cell phones, the police found a single green-sequined slipper lying on the steps, in a kind of sick echo of *Cinderella*. But there was no question of finding the foot it would properly fit: Samantha's was still snuggled inside.

Laughter

A summer spent in Ireland turned out to be every bit as dull as Shaun O'Malley had expected. He was stuck with his family on his great-grandmother's little farm outside the fishing village of Skibbereen. His father, head writer for the teenage TV comedy series *Make Me!*, was trying to write a serious novel based on his family's Irish history. Shaun's mother, who was also a writer, was working on a book of travel essays. Both hoped to use the summer to "soak up local color." As far as Shaun was concerned, the whole experience bit the big one.

His relatives drove him up the wall. His great–grandmother Tessie was forever boring him with stories about banshees and pookas—some kind of goblins that ran around in the shape of a fire-eyed horse—and crap. Mostly she talked about the "Good Folk" or "Little People," who would give a blessing or make mischief, depending on how they were treated.

Shaun, who had been rolling his eyes at his parents across the breakfast table, said in as bored a tone as he could manage, "You mean fairies, don't you, Great-Gran Tessie?"

"Hush!" the woman said, glancing around as if she expected to see an elf peeking out of a cupboard or popping up out of the fruit bowl on the sideboard. "Never say that! You offend them if you name them directly. You don't want to risk that."

"Fairies! Fairies! Fairies!—*Phooey!* I don't believe in them—and why call them 'good' if they do stuff that hurts people? This is all too loony tunes," said the boy. "Pookas and fairies—*get real!*" He began to laugh.

"You should learn to show some respect, young Shaun," said his great-grandmother, "for your elders and for them as you may not see, but who are near. Careless laughter may come back to haunt you."

"Shaun!" said his father, goaded into action. "Apologize to Tessie now."

"Sorry," he said, in his most insincere voice.

His great-grandmother, still angry, began to clear the breakfast dishes. Shaun's mother jumped up to help.

"Well, back to work," said his father, standing up. "I think I've got that plot problem sorted out." He leaned over and whispered to Shaun, "Chill a little."

"Couldn't we go home, or at least to a *hotel?* They're driving me *nuts.*"

"This is a once-in-a-lifetime opportunity," said his father.

"Yeah, 'cause it's gonna kill me," Shaun muttered as his father left.

If Tessie bored him with her stories, then her sons, Shaun's great-uncles, put him over the edge with their endless efforts to become his pals. Riley and Dooley (Shaun had unkindly called them "Rufus" and "Doofus," until his father, in a rare assertive moment, had forbidden him to use the nicknames), always wanted to take him fishing (a big *Ugh!* to him) on the nearby Branny River, which he thought looked more like a creek. To Shaun, the sad little stream barely looked able to produce minnows. Worse, the men wanted to teach him the art of snaring rabbits (*Double-ugh!* in his mind). He spent a good part of his days avoiding them. He was glad when duties around the farm kept them occupied from sunrise to sundown, leaving him free to wander or laze on his own.

What was the pits to him was heaven to his parents. They kept saying how "inspired" he ought to be as they dragged him on an endless round of visits to country churches and cemeteries, to crystal and linen shops and factories, and to storytelling and folksinging festivals, where he barely understood a tenth of what was said or sung— and cared even less.

His only real enjoyment was playing practical jokes on his two great-uncles, whom he considered dimwits. He unlatched the gate of the pigpen, acting surprised when the brothers came in to dinner covered with mud and grime from chasing down the escaped swine. He hid tools and again claimed innocence. But he was caught when he glued the fingers of their work gloves together with some Super glue he had brought from home. Still, the halfhearted lecture from his parents, while his great-uncles and great-grandmother sat watching like a judge and jury, only made him more determined to find other—if subtler—ways to irritate his kin and so amuse himself.

"I'm only joking," he protested, when his father warned him to stop his mischief-making. "What's wrong with laughing a little? Everyone's so serious around here."

"There's a time and a place for laughter," his great-grandmother pronounced.

"Anytime and anyplace seem fine to me," said Shaun.

"You're hopeless," said his father. But the boy could see that his parent was trying to hide a grin of his own. And his mother's eyes had the sparkle he recognized as concealed amusement. They didn't care, Shaun realized. He'd get all the laughs he wanted. He suddenly snorted at the absurdity of it all: his mother and father like prosecuting attorneys and his relatives like judge and jury accusing him of—*laughing!* In his mind his grandmother suddenly took on the shape of the Red Queen in *Alice in Wonderland.* Everyone in the room became a Wonderland figure in his mind.

"Off with my head!" he shouted. He nearly doubled over with laughter. "The boy is too happy to live!"

His parents cracked up at this. The disapproval of his great-uncles and great-grandmother only made the other three laugh more loudly. Finally, taking off his glasses and wiping tears from his eyes, Shaun's father said, "Sorry! Sorry! But what are you going to do with a kid who's too smart for his own good?"

Dooley pointed his finger at his grandnephew: "Have a care you don't laugh your foolish head off someday."

"I heard of a man started laughing one day and couldn't stop," warned Riley. "He couldn't eat or drink or sleep for all the laughing. T'were the end of him. But they say you can still hear him laughing in his grave at night. They say he angered the Good Folk."

"Oh, *please!*" Shaun said. "Those old stories! And Great-Gran says swallowing gum will gum up my insides, and doing this . . ." He made a face with eyes crossed. ". . . will make my face freeze that way. Those are stories no one believes. You guys really need to get a life. I'm going to bed." He beat a hasty retreat to his room, realizing he'd probably gone way beyond what was acceptable even to his easygoing parents.

His bedroom was upstairs. It had two windows in the corner, since it was itself tucked into the corner of the second story. To the south was a glimpse of distant, blue-green sea. To the west was a meadow with a bit of forest. The only thing of interest was what seemed to be the ruins of a castle, on a stretch of hillside surrounded by trees. But when he had proposed, in a rare moment of friendship, that his great-uncles take him exploring there, they had glanced worriedly at each other, then refused.

114

Dooley had explained, "That up high is a 'rath,' a place where the Good Folk gather on some days or nights to dance and sing and feast. You don't want to be disturbin' them."

His brother had added, "The Little People can be bad-tempered, if you trespass on their doin's or show them disrespect."

Sometimes he would dream of the Good People, dancing in a circle around his room or over his head. Though he didn't believe in them, it kept the idea of visiting the ruins in front of his waking mind.

Shaun had asked his uncles several more times, and they always refused. This just added to his resentment of the superstitious twosome. He got a vague promise or two from his father to go exploring, but the man always seemed to have reached some crucial point in his writing or had some boring place to visit for research.

So Shaun had made up his mind to go exploring on his own. Now, in his room, listening to the others settle down, he realized that the events of the day and the evening's "trial" had charged him up. He wasn't sleepy in the least. Outside the full moon had turned the fields and meadows to sheets of bright silver. He opened the window and found that the air was unusually warm. It seemed a perfect night for an adventure.

Far in the distance, the ruins of the "rath" looked like a tumble of silver stones. It was like a beacon there on the far hillside, calling to him.

Slipping on his nylon Windbreaker and taking a couple

of candy bars for the trip, he slid out of his window, tiptoed across the gently sloping roof, and, using the bathroom drainpipe, lowered himself to the ground. He'd discovered this secret way in and out of his room while playing tricks on his uncles.

It took him a lot longer to reach the place than he expected. And the last twenty minutes of climbing to the shattered fortress was more nerve-racking than he could have guessed. The slope was far steeper than it looked from his window. But when he was only a few feet below the outer circle of tumbled stone, he heard faint music, like bells and fiddles and flutes, and high, piping laughter.

Was it possible that the tales about the Good Folk could be true? he wondered. More afraid of scaring the creatures away—if they existed—than of any danger, he made the last climb as quietly as possible.

He crept through a gap in the wall and then followed a second bit of wall, taller than his head, to the right. Another opening—this one had clearly been a door—led him to a second passage, where the sound of the music and revelry drew him now to the left. Some fifty feet along, he came to an archway. Peering cautiously around the corner, he breathed a silent "Wow!" at the sight.

The courtyard beyond was filled with scattered stones, clearly tumbled from the surrounding walls. But, at the center of the moonlit open space, an area had been cleared for a dance floor. There a sea of tiny figures, all clothed in green, advanced and bowed, retreated and spun, formed lines and circles, linked arms and parted, following the steps and patterns of a dizzyingly complex dance. On the far side of the ring, tiny musicians played a strange and frenzied tune. Seated on a tall rock above them was a figure wrapped in a green cloak edged in what seemed to be rabbit fur, with a gold crown tilted slightly on his head.

But it wasn't the fact that these creatures truly existed that fascinated Shaun: it was the look of them. The pictures he'd seen in books of fairy tales always showed them as handsome or slightly comical creatures, but appealing and well-proportioned. Yet what he saw by moonlight was very different. These creatures looked as though a careless child had assembled them from an endless supply of broken dolls and toys. Arms and legs were mismatched, so many of the creatures limped and lumbered in time to the music. Heads too big for bodies seemed in danger of crashing to the earth when a dancer bowed to his or her partner. Eyes were of the wrong sizes; noses were set off-center; mouths grinned or gaped foolishly to reveal gaps between teeth or spots where a missing tooth had been replaced with a stone or a seed or a broken bit of pottery. Some were bald, while others had hair that bristled like brooms or jutted out like springs from a broken couch. Even the king, perched upon his high stone, looked like Mr. Potato Head to Shaun.

They were so funny-looking and ungainly, Shaun couldn't help himself: he began to giggle. Though he pressed his hands to his mouth to choke back the laughter, he couldn't contain himself.

The small merrymakers heard. At a sudden signal from the king, the music ceased; the dancers froze in place.

"'Twould seem we have us a visitor," said the king, his voice surprisingly loud coming from one so small. "Come forth, whoever ye be."

There was a power in the voice that frightened Shaun, even as it compelled him—against his will—to reveal himself to the Little People.

"Step forward, lad," the king commanded, crooking his finger at Shaun. Each time he bent his finger, the boy was tugged forward, like a fish being reeled in on an invisible line.

Nothing seemed very funny now. He walked forward like a broken, resistant puppet, controlled by the king. The dancers parted silently before him. He felt like Moses as the ankle-deep sea of grotesque, clumsy figures made way for him. At last he stood before the king, who was eye-to-eye with him because of the height of the stone on which the bulbous figure sat.

"So ye like to laugh," said the king of the fairies.

Fearfully, Shaun nodded.

"And just what was it you were findin' so provokin'?" the little man asked slyly.

"You were having such a good time," Shaun said quickly. "I was just having fun seeing you have fun."

"Were ye now?" said the king. Then he stood upon the rock and shouted to the waiting dancers and musicians, "The lad here meant no disrespect—"

Shaun shook his head.

"And his bit o' trespassin' tonight, well, it's no harm done t' the likes o' us."

118

The others remained silent, watchful.

"Now laughter can be a blessin', and we likes t' laugh ourselves, so let's all have a good laugh." With that he put his hands on his hips and threw back his head and began to laugh uproariously. And the crowd of Good Folk laughed, too. The sound of their merriment filled the courtyard. And it was so contagious that Shaun forgot his fear and joined in their laughter.

"Oh, lad," said the king, wiping tears of glee off his cheeks and at last getting control of himself. "It's a heartfelt moment o' joy ye've brought us. So we must give ye somethin' in return. Now you're a high-spirited lad who loves to laugh. Well, laugh ye will, laugh ye shall: for the rest of your life, ye'll have merriment and to spare."

At his signal, the fairy musicians began to play, the dancers rejoined the dance, and the king indicated that Shaun, whose sides ached from all the laughing, should sit below him, his back to the high stone, and enjoy the revels from the seat of honor.

But watching the dancers and listening to the strange music suddenly made the boy very tired. He fought to keep his eyes open, but he was soon fast asleep.

Awaking in the first light of dawn, he felt cold and cramped and out of sorts. The events of the night before seemed nothing more than a dream. Had he seen anything? he wondered. Or had he just fallen asleep and dreamed it all?

He knew he was going to be in big trouble for going off in the middle of the night. Though his dream had been all about laughter, nothing seemed very funny about the way he felt and the hassle that was sure to follow his return.

Halfway home, he was found by his great-uncle Dooley, who was heading one of several hastily formed search parties.

His parents and relatives were relieved to find him safe and sound, but they were angry about all the worry and effort he had caused them.

"Where in heaven's name *were* you?" his father asked, after concerned friends and neighbors had left and there was just the family sitting in the parlor. Sitting on a kitchen chair and flanked by his parents, Shaun felt like a prisoner under guard. Uncle Dooley leaned against the mantle; Uncle Riley sat on one of the two big armchairs that were the small room's main furnishings. Great-Gran Tessie sat across from him, looking more than ever like a very unamused queen.

"I couldn't sleep. I went to the 'rath'—that old place up on the hill."

"Sure an' you didn't!" cried Dooley, leaning forward, looking startled.

"Sure an' I *did*," the boy snapped back. "And I saw—or I thought I saw—the fairies." (He ignored the sudden gasps of his great-grandmother and great-uncles when he named the creatures directly.) "Anyhow, they weren't so bad. They heard me laugh, and that sorta got them laughing, too."

"It was a dream," said his mother. "You fell asleep and dreamed it all."

"There are no such things as fa—as the Good Folk," said his father, catching Tessie's warning glance.

"It sure seemed real." Suddenly he had a vision of the broken-doll dancers, distorted musicians, and the crowned Mr. Potato Head. The memory rushed over him as if he were back in the moonlit courtyard. They looked so silly and clumsy and . . .

Shaun got a fresh fit of the giggles.

Dooley said, "The lad may have been touched by the Good Folk."

"You're the ones who are touched—*in the head,*" sputtered Shaun, as his giggles turned to helpless laughter. His guffaws came louder and louder. Everywhere he looked he saw tiny goggle-eyed, clubfooted, twisted-mouthed, swollen-headed folk, all roaring with laughter. They fed his own merriment.

"Everything's a joke to that lad," said Riley in disgust, getting up to leave. "Well, go on, young Shaun, laugh your head off."

Which, to everyone's astonishment, is just what happened.

Still grinning, it rolled to a stop at Great-Gran Tessie's feet.

Click-Clack

"**D**on't go into the woods after dark," the kids at Forest Estates Middle School would warn new students. "Something there doesn't like people."

Before developers cut the land into plots and started building houses, the 1,000-acre woods had been private property, belonging to the wealthy Uberholzer family. Now less than half the forest remained. But it was the source of countless stories. In addition to rumors of a monster, there were stories that remnants of the fierce Taweskanni tribe had been wiped out by a war party of Mohawk, Seneca, and Oneida warriors. The ghosts of the lost tribe reportedly still haunted the woods.

Though their parents laughed off such tales of ghastly

creatures or ghostly Indians, the kids of Forest Estates knew better. Little kids who played near the chain-link fence that divided the houses and yards from the woods talked of hearing murmurs and whispers and even seeing shadowy shapes in the green shade. One child swore he had glimpsed something like a giant caterpillar; but he made up so many stories no one believed him.

Older kids who dared to climb the fence in sunlight to explore the forest told of finding the prints of moccasins or places where bushes and branches were broken in a way that suggested something far bigger than a man had pushed through the trees. They swore they had heard weird cries coming from deep among the trees.

Every child was curious to know the solution to the mystery, but none wanted to come face-to-face with the answer.

Zach Quinn certainly didn't. But when his older friend, Bruce Baylor, dared him to go exploring with him one afternoon, he was more afraid of being laughed at and losing Bruce's friendship than of running into something in the sunlit woods. So he followed the older boy over the fence when they were sure no one was watching.

Bruce was reckless. Zach envied his friend's daring yet feared where he might lead them. But Bruce only had to mutter the word "Chicken," and Zach had no choice but to follow.

Their explorations took them into the woods beyond a point any other kids had boasted of reaching. But when Zach suggested returning, Bruce insisted, "Just a little farther." When they'd been roaming for almost two hours, Bruce discovered what seemed to be a deer trail. They decided to follow it through the thicket, until it led them to a primitive cabin. It was surrounded by brush, and the roof looked like nothing more than a mass of fallen branches and leaves. If they hadn't passed within a few feet of it, they never would have seen it amid the dense trees. It looked long abandoned. Curious, they were trying to peer through a dust-encrusted window when the owner, a thin, gray-haired woman in a ragged print dress, opened the door quite unexpectedly.

"Come in, you boys," she called. "Come in." To Zach, her words sounded like a command.

Clearly curious, Bruce shrugged, then whispered, "Stay near the door in case she's as crazy as she looks. Remember the movie about the woman who had the loony son? She'd lure folks inside, and he'd finish them off."

"Give it a rest," said Zach, trying to sound braver than he felt. "You're just trying to creep me out." He followed the other boy into the house. When his sun-dazzled eyes adjusted to the gloom, he found himself in a small room furnished with odds and ends of furniture so that it looked like a junk shop.

"We didn't think anyone lived here," Zach explained.

"Well, someone does. I'm Rosa Moline. One time, I was a maid at the Uberholzer mansion—before they turned it into a fancy country club for all these newcomers. I'm part Indian. I like living by myself. I live off what the forest provides."

"I thought this was private property," said Bruce. "Doesn't it belong to some big company now? The one that built Forest Estates?"

Click-Clack

"I worked a lifetime for the Uberholzers," she said, sounding angry. "Don't that give me the right to live here?"

"Oh, sure," Zach said quickly, signaling Bruce to play along. Then he added, "We heard there were ghosts or something in these woods. You ever see anything scary?"

She answered vaguely, "Nothing bothers poor old Rosa Moline." Then she picked up two pale, polished stones in the palm of her left hand. They had a faintly yellowish cast, like old ivory or bone, thought Zach. He thought they might be some kind of worry beads, like the ones his math teacher at school used. Mrs. Abrams said moving them around in her hand relaxed her. *Click-clack, click-clack.* The old woman worked the stones faster and faster.

Her voice grew angrier. "I live in peace here. But now noisy, nosy children come looking, looking—though no one has found me until today."

Uncomfortable at her tone, which seemed almost menacing now, Zach looked around for his friend. But Bruce had forgotten his own advice. Intrigued by a shelf full of Indian arrowheads, baskets, and other dusty items, he had wandered away from the door to the other end of the room. Zach took a step backward, when the threat in the woman's voice suddenly became undeniable as she muttered, "I can't let you leave now. The world thinks Rosa Moline is dead. People have forgotten me. It's best that way."

The stones *click-clack*ed at a furious pace now. *"Bruce!"* hissed Zach. "We're outta here!"

But his friend, fascinated by the arrowheads he was examining, ignored him.

Click-clack. Clickety-clack. The stones in the old woman's bony fingers were moving faster, filling the cabin with their sound.

Suddenly, she began to change. Her body grew long and twisty. Her arms lengthened, ending now in talons that repeated the *click-clack* of the stones that she dropped on the dirty wooden floor. Rosa Moline's jaws became like a snake's, snapping open and shut rapidly, making a chattering sound. But the distorted features were still recognizable as Rosa's.

"Bruce!" Zach yelled. The other boy, intent on slipping several arrowheads and a bead necklace into his pocket, spun around, sending a pottery dish filled with what looked like seeds crashing to the floor. The monster roared, turning its full attention on Bruce. The boy screamed, scrambling backward so hastily that he tripped over a stack of kindling and went down with a bone-jarring *thud.* The snake-woman's tail lashed out, circled the bellowing boy's ankles, and yanked him close. Now he was screaming, "Zach! Help me!"

But Zach could think only about saving himself. He wrenched open the front door and ran for his life. Behind him, he could hear his friend screaming for help, but self-preservation was his only thought. He ran, not caring in which direction he headed, wanting only to put as much distance as possible between himself and the horror in the cabin. He was thankful that the massed trees and brush soon swallowed his friend's shrieks as he plunged deeper into the woods.

Click-Clack

Then his foot caught in the twisted root of a tree. He crashed down, hearing the sickening *crack* of bone, feeling a searing pain in his ankle. Sobbing with hurt, panic, and exhaustion, he tugged his foot free. The process was so agonizing, he was sure he had broken a bone.

The forest suddenly went deathly still. Behind him, he heard a teasing, deadly *click-clack*.

Whimpering, he tried to crawl away from the sound. But it drew relentlessly nearer. Knowing he couldn't escape, Zach scrambled into the thickest patch of brush he could find. He quieted his gasps by breathing as shallowly as he could. Maybe, just maybe, he could hide from the Rosa-thing.

Something pushed clumsily through the underbrush. Mixed in with the *snap-crackle* of dry leaves and twigs was the awful *click-clack*. The thing passed his hiding place, moved deeper into the woods, then stopped.

Zach held his breath for as long as possible.

"Found you!" a familiar voice yelled, as the branches in front of him were thrust aside.

Zach screeched in shock and terror, even as he recognized Bruce's face grinning down at him.

"What's the matter, Zach? Scared of an old friend?" Bruce looked down at Zach's rapidly swelling ankle. "Poor Zach. Looks like you hurt yourself."

Something in the other boy's tone angered Zach, who was still frightened and feeling sorry for himself. "I *am* hurt. Stop making fun of me. Give me a hand. We've got to get away before—" He stopped suddenly. "How did you escape?"

"I sure didn't have any help from you," said Bruce, making no effort to take Zach's outstretched hand or help his friend. He just kept grinning.

Zach looked closer. There was something wrong with Bruce's face, he realized. It looked longer. His whole body—what Zach could see of it—looked thinner. It was as if all his bones had been compressed and rearranged. He looked *squeezed* into a taller, narrower version of himself. Zach suddenly remembered reading in a book about snakes of how an anaconda or boa would crush its prey in its coils before devouring the victim.

"Where's the old lady? That . . . *thing?*" Zach asked, his voice little more than a whisper now.

"She's back at the cabin. She's old. She's tired. She needs someone to help her."

"Help *me*," Zach pleaded.

"Why should I? You didn't give a thought to me a little while ago."

Zach couldn't say anything. Tears were running down his cheeks now, but he felt too weak to lift his hand to wipe them away as they dribbled off his chin. He remembered another thing from his reading: how snakes are supposed to be able to hypnotize their prey by staring at them. Of course, the book explained, they don't really hypnotize their victims. It's just that the rabbit or mouse or whatever is so terrified at confronting the predator that it freezes in fear.

Even the pain in his broken ankle faded as Zach saw the other boy, who was and wasn't Bruce, lift his hand to show the two pale, polished stones in his palm.

Click-Clack

Click-clack.

Click.

Clack.

One after the other, the stones hit the ground as Bruce's hands turned into claws at the ends of his lengthening arms.

The grinning face in front of Zach split wide into jaws big enough to swallow a person.

And they did.

Daddy Boogey

$\mathbf{S}$even-year-old Andy loved going to Nebraska to see his grandparents. The town of Pickard was a million miles from any big city, but it was fun to be away from everyday things like mowing the lawn, choir practice, cleaning up dog poop. Getting there wasn't much fun; on the plane, he always had to sit with his sister and mother, while they talked about girl stuff. His brothers, Rob and Mitch, fourteen and fifteen, sat with their dad and talked sports and fishing and other cool things.

But he really liked his grandparents, his mother's folks. Their stories about early days on the farm were mixed with exciting stories about even earlier times, when the first settlers came to the area. If the talk veered off into boring subjects—like the weather and what the corn crop would bring, or how much an acre the people down the road got for selling their farm to something called an "agribusiness"—Andy could steer it back by asking a question about the old days.

The only problem was the house, where he had to sleep in the third-floor room with his brothers. At home he had a room to himself. But here he shared space in the big room that was always just called "the attic." And that's what it had been: a big open space with walls and ceiling covered in plywood, a floor covered in old green linoleum with lots of chunks gouged out of it, and three beds, three dressers, and three lamps as furnishings. Two-thirds of the upstairs space was bedroom; the remaining third was left as storage space, closed off by a big square door of raw plywood set in a wall of unpainted Sheetrock at the end of the room. Inside was a cramped space where all the junk that had once been in the whole attic was now stored. Dusty light sifted through an old window with a broken latch that sometimes banged faintly on windy nights. Every summer Andy mentioned this to his grandfather, but somehow the man never got around to fixing it. Every now and then, Andy was sure he could hear things moving around behind the closed door—rats or squirrels or . . . Well, he didn't know what, but he always made sure the hook and eye latch that secured the door was in place, even though his older brothers called him a "crybaby" for being so afraid.

In the sleeping area there was one big window that

looked out across the shingle roof to the cornfields and the town of Pickard down the road; a smaller window opposite, above the stairwell, was so high and small it offered a view only of the Nebraska sky.

The only other thing that bothered him were the old-fashioned scarecrows his grandpa insisted on scattering around the cornfields. Most were far enough away to look like nothing more than dolls. But there was one in the field across the road that seemed too lifelike, too watchful. He'd gone to see it up close when he'd first noticed it last summer. It was put together of old burlap bags stuffed with straw. The hands were gnarly branches. His grandfather had painted the face with big googly eyes and a grin that was, Andy guessed, supposed to look clownish and funny, but just looked *creepy*. No matter where he stood, the eyes seemed to follow him, like the ones in paintings he'd seen for sale at a souvenir shop in Portland, where the family lived.

He made a point of not going near the scarecrow again, but his brothers sensed his reluctance. They named the scarecrow "Daddy Boogey" and made up stories about how it would come alive on nights when the moon was full and bursting with magic or when lightning from summer storms charged it like Frankenstein's monster.

The more Andy begged them to stop, the more frequent and horrible their stories became. "There was a van full of kids coming back from choir practice at the Baptist church," said Rob. "They swear something tall and scraggly came running out of the cornfields onto the highway and chased them for a mile, running as fast as the car was going. It kept trying to pound in the back window—even rode the bumper for a while. The driver freaked and swerved and the thing flew off. No one can say for sure what it was, but there were these twigs in the rubber all around the back window—just like Daddy Boogey's fingers had snapped off, trying to pry it open."

"No one wants to tell you, because you're so little and such a scaredy-cat," Mitch said, "but there was a farm hand who made fun of the scarecrow, saying how lousy Grandpa had made it. He disappeared about a year ago. They found him wired onto a scarecrow's pole in the McGintys' corn-field. His mouth and nose and ears were stuffed full of hay, so he suffocated. I guess he wasn't much of a scarecrow, 'cause the birds had pecked out his eyes."

"I know you're just making this stuff up!" yelled Andy. "I'm going to tell Mom, if you keep trying to scare me."

"*I'm going to te-ell. I'm going to te-ell,*" his brothers mim-icked. "What a baby!"

He knew what they were up to, but the truth was that the stories *did* scare him, a little. Sometimes, from the attic bedroom, he'd watch the scarecrow. It seemed to shiver and jitter in the afternoon heat-shimmers; at night, he some-times thought it was waving to him. Oh, he was sure it was only the wind and the moonlight playing tricks. *Probably.* But it was easy to imagine the thing shambling across the nighttime fields, climbing up the oak tree, and letting itself through the unlatched attic window into the house.

*　　*　　*

They had been there less than a week when what had been a sunny day turned to gray in the evening with the threat of a summer storm. Andy's mother sent him to find his brothers and call them in to dinner. He found the older boys in the cornfield on the far side of the road, shying stones at Daddy Boogey. They had shattered most of one branch hand and burst the cheek below the painted right eye, so hay was sticking out.

"Mom says you gotta come to dinner," Andy said, adding, "Grandpa won't like you doing that."

"He'll think it just happened," said Rob.

"Unless someone tells," Mitch added nastily.

"I'm not going to tell," their younger brother said quickly. "I wouldn't care if the stupid thing got wrecked. I hate it."

"Shhhh!" said Rob, finger to his lips. He stood on tiptoe and pretended to put his hands over the scarecrow's non-existent ears. "He might hear you and get mad."

"Yeah!" said Mitch. "You wouldn't want to make him mad. He might come and *GETCHA!*" Yelling this last word, he grabbed Andy. *"Daddy Boogey attack!"* Rob joined in the tussle, tickling Andy until he begged them to stop. They did: by dumping him into the dirt between two rows of corn. Then they ran off, leaving the boy gasping for breath.

Andy was suddenly aware of how dark the sky had become; a rising wind set the cornstalks shivering and whispering. As he brushed himself off, he noticed that the setting sun, visible in a band of red light beneath a ceiling of slate-colored clouds, had thrown the scarecrow's long shadow halfway to the road. He looked up, expecting to see the

136

painted eyes staring at him, following him, but against the setting sun the scarecrow was just a black figure with a broken hand and a head tilted to one side by Rob's or Mitch's lucky throw.

Feeling very small and alone, Andy began to run after his brothers.

The storm broke while they were having dinner. Lightning flashed behind sheets of rain and gusts of wind. The power dipped once or twice, dimming the lights, but it didn't fail. Still, Andy, who always wanted to know that he could turn on the lamp on the dresser, asked whether he could keep a flashlight by his bed, just in case. His brothers—and even his sister—started teasing him about being "afraid of the dark and Daddy Boogey," until their parents put a stop to it. Grandpa went and fetched an extra flashlight, but it wasn't working.

"I meant to buy extra batteries when I was in town," Grandpa confessed. "You'll just have to hope the power don't go down altogether."

"Could I have some candles then?" he asked, remembering that he had seen some emergency candles in a kitchen drawer.

"No," said his mother. "It's too dangerous unless an adult lights them."

He tried to argue the point but failed.

Still, before he went to bed, he slipped the candles out of the kitchen and took them upstairs in his pants pocket. He knew there was an old ashtray in the drawer of his dresser that he could stand a candle in, if he needed to. He hated disobeying, but he couldn't face the thought of getting through the night without a light. As long as the power held, there was a night light to brighten the steep stairs from the attic to the second floor landing. It kept a comforting soft glow in the big sleeping area. Andy hated that his bed was in the darkest corner of the big room, between the storage space door and the window facing toward town. But the night light and the knowledge that his brothers—for all they teased him—were sleeping in the twin beds on the other side of the room helped keep most of his night fears at a low level.

By the time he was ready for bed the storm was at full tilt. He could hear the wind-tossed oak tree scraping against the storage room wall. The loose window made a soft *whump-whump-whump* beyond the plywood door. Kneeling on the end of his bed, he looked out at the nearest scarecrow, but it was nothing more than a dark blot against the night, further hidden by heavy rain. Then a flash of lightning showed it twisting in the wind; in his imagination, it was trying to twist itself free of its pole. That idea and the thunderclap that followed sent him diving under the covers.

He touched the drawer that held the candles: *just in case*. He heard his brothers murmuring and laughing—probably telling dirty jokes. Their voices, the scratching oak, and the soft thumping of the window blended together into a soft buzz, and he fell asleep.

Andy wasn't sure what woke him up, but something felt wrong. Right away he noticed that the night light was out.

IIe guessed the power had failed. The storm had quieted somewhat. Keeping a blanket wrapped around him, he crawled on his knees to the window. The lightning seemed to have moved far to the south, beyond the town of Pickard. But the town itself was completely dark, so the power was off there, too.

There was a sudden groan, choked off, from one of his brothers. Rob or Mitch must be having a nightmare. *Good!* thought Andy, *serves them right for trying to scare me earlier!* Then came a second sound—like a gasp that suddenly became a gurgle. Then there was a thrashing sound, like one of the boys kicking his bed. Then a silence so complete, Andy couldn't hear Rob's soft snoring or Mitch's breathing. Their half of the room was black without the night light's glow.

"Guys!" hissed Andy. "You awake?"

There was a rustling sound from across the room. Then a sudden *bang!* that made him shout. The storage room door had been partway open and had suddenly slammed shut. *But how could it be open?* he wondered. He had double-checked the hook and eye as he did every night. Someone from downstairs—maybe his grandpa—must have come upstairs to get something and had forgotten to close the door afterwards. *BANG!* The door was thrown open by another gust of wind—a strong blast. The attic window must be wide-open.

There was more rustling, a little nearer now, but still in darkness.

Then a distant flash of lightning lit the room briefly. There was someone standing between the other boys' beds, his back to the main part of the room. "Dad? Grandpa?" called Andy.

Something rustled like dried grass. *Like hay.* A shape was moving across the room towards him. "Dad?" he asked again, but it wasn't so much a question as a plea.

Now he could see the manlike figure halfway across the darkened room. Backing himself up against the headboard of the old-fashioned bed, Andy slid the drawer open and found one of the emergency candles and the box of kitchen matches he had also taken. For a moment, he was afraid to light the candle, for fear of what he would see. But he knew he would pass out from fright if he had to face the shape in total darkness.

The match flared, and he lit the small white candle, holding it out in front of him like a weapon.

Daddy Boogey was only a few feet from the bed! The thing suddenly drew back a step in the candle's glow. The terrifying clown face seemed swollen to twice its size in the wildly flickering light. The eyes—somehow terribly alive—were riveted on the tiny flame. The thing took a sliding step closer, then stopped again, eyes locked on the candle.

It's afraid of fire, thought Andy. He remembered the scene in *The Wizard of Oz* where the witch tried to set the frantic Scarecrow aflame. Holding the lit candle out with his left hand, Andy fumbled another candle out of the drawer with his right hand. He lit the second one from the first. Daddy Boogey took a big step back.

"Leave me alone, or I'll burn you up," said Andy, trying to sound brave but knowing he sounded more like the

scared little kid he was. "Go away!" The scarecrow paused and seemed to be considering what to do. Holding the candles out, imagining they were twin lightsabers from a *Star Wars* movie, Andy scooted closer on his knees. He called to his brothers, but they didn't answer. He guessed they were huddled in the far corner of the room or hiding under their beds, watching Andy stand off Daddy Boogey in the circle of candlelight.

"Mom! Dad! Grandpa!" Andy tried to yell, but his throat was so dry, the words sounded like a frog's croaking —something that couldn't be heard downstairs with the wind and rain slamming the house.

He would try to back the scarecrow away with the fire, until he could get to the stairs. Then he'd run and wake up the household.

But just as he started to put his foot down on the floor, the storage room door burst open, and a gust of damp air rushed through the room and extinguished the light of his candles.

He heard the scarecrow shuffling toward him; in a flash of lightning, he saw it reaching for him. Having no other choice, he turned and yanked at the edge of the sliding-glass window over his bed, wrenching it so hard, the glass panel jammed partway open. Branchy fingers caught in his hair, clutched at the shoulder of his P.J.'s. He threw himself forward, popping the flyscreen and sending it scuttling across the shingles to disappear over the edge of the roof.

He kicked like a wild man and flung his head from side

to side, tearing his hair free of the nightmare fingers. The other hand, which had been grasping his shoulder, had a weaker grip, probably because that was the hand that his brothers had broken earlier. In an instant, he was through the window and rolling down the rain-slicked shingles, scrabbling with his hands to slow himself before he followed the flyscreen over the eaves and into a three-story drop.

His toes caught in the rain gutter, filled with freezing water. His nails dug into the water-softened wood of the roof. He was safe for the moment.

The window above him was filled with the scarecrow's moon face as the two arms reached for him. For an instant he thought the thing would follow him onto the roof, but it retreated. Not taking a chance, the boy crawled as far away as he could get, finding a little shelter from the rain and wind beside the brick chimney. He couldn't tell where his shivering from the cold left off and his shivering from fright began. He huddled in misery.

When he couldn't bear the wet and chill any longer, he made his way carefully to the broken window. Every second he expected the grinning, staring sack face to appear. But when he looked in, to his surprise he saw what seemed like an empty room. Scarcely daring to breathe, he climbed as quietly through the window as he could.

The storage room door was ajar. He had the sudden fear that Daddy Boogey might be hiding inside, waiting in ambush for him. But though the door gave one heart-wrenching, wind-driven lurch, no monster appeared. Both rooms were truly deserted.

Too deserted: Rob and Mitch were gone. They must have fled downstairs. But if that were the case, why weren't the adults up and rushing to Andy's rescue?

On impulse, he looked out the window toward the cornfield.

The last lightning flash of the storm lit up the rows of corn.

Lit up the *three* figures fastened to the scarecrow's pole.

This time Andy's screams were plenty loud enough to wake up the folks downstairs.

Grey

"Grey was the scariest movie monster of all time," said Alec Pardo, slowing the car as traffic began to back up near the end of the San Mateo Bridge, connecting the peninsula below San Francisco with the East Bay area.

Nancy Kim, sitting beside him in the front seat, said, "That was his name? Just 'Grey'?"

"Well, sometimes he was called 'Mr. Grey' or 'Grey Master' or something like that. Of course, we're talking about silent movies, so you'd just see it printed on a card in between shots."

In the backseat of the car, Alec's twelve-year-old sister, Alana, adjusted her headphones and pumped up the music on her CD player. Talk about old movies bored her as much as it turned her older brother on. She was annoyed to find that her best friend, Nancy, was genuinely interested. She had invited Nancy along to keep her company, but her friend was caught up in Alec's tiresome talk about silent movies and old film stars and movie studios that had gone out of business countless years ago.

Alana had heard it all too many times before. It was the curse of having a brother working on his master's degree at the San Francisco Film Academy and two parents involved in the business; their father was director of photography, their mother was a special effects makeup artist. In fact, Alec was taking care of his younger sister while their folks were working on *Alien Abduction: Part II,* on location in New Mexico. Their mom had created the creepy "alien greys" for the original film and now was making the latex monsters even creepier for the sequel.

As part of his study of filmmaking in the San Francisco area, Alec often visited the sites of the old studios—all long gone except for an occasional building or historical marker. But Alec liked to "soak up the atmosphere, get a feel for the old places." So today they were taking a long, dull drive to the town of Dunham, where what was left of the old SSGG Studios could be found. "The letters stood for *Silver Screen Golden Gate,*" Alec had explained to Nancy earlier, while his sister, in the backseat, tried to keep from shouting, "Who cares?" Movies, to her, were something you did for fun or, in their parents' case, to earn a living. They were *not* something you studied and talked about as if they were *religious experiences.*

146

Grey

"Are we there yet?" Alana asked, deliberately sounding as backseat-bratty as she could.

"Not much longer," her brother said good-naturedly. "There's the Dunham exit ahead." They made the turn and were soon following the road to the town tucked back in the hills burned brown by the summer heat.

"What made this Grey guy so scary?" asked Nancy.

"That's hard to say, exactly," Alec replied. "None of the movies still exist; all the masters and most copies went up in smoke during the fire that destroyed SSGG Studios in 1928. There were twelve Grey movies made, plus one that was never released. Supposedly unlucky number thirteen was so scary, the studio felt it might frighten some people to death. According to the old stories, even August McGuire, who founded the studio—he was sometimes called 'Moneygrubbing McGuire'—was willing to keep the film from being shown, because it was too awful. I guess it's sort of like when that studio kept the old movie *Freaks* from being shown, because people might be so grossed out."

"Don't movie people always use ads that say how horrible and disgusting scary films are to get people to come?" Nancy wondered.

"That's kind of a modern idea. But even back in the fifties and sixties they'd sometimes have nurses in the lobby of the theater or make people sign a paper saying they wouldn't sue if they suffered shock, or sometimes they even promised money to the survivors of anyone who died of fright. Those were all gimmicks."

They were passing through the sleepy little town of

Dunham, rolling along tree-shaded streets, heading into the canyon beyond that housed the old studio.

"But Grey seems to have been something different," Alec continued. "For one thing, he seemed to be able to scare everyone. But people could never say exactly what had frightened them so much. In fact, Grey seemed to take different shapes in different films, or even in the same film. They were all black-and-white back then, but people would talk about grey mist or a grey man or a grey vampire. No two could agree on exactly what they thought they'd seen."

"Weird," said Nancy.

"There was even a theory that the movies used some form of subliminal perception . . ."

"Huh?"

"Secret messages hidden in the film that flashed by too fast for people to realize, even though they got the meaning at some unconscious level. It supposedly worked like hypnosis. They tried it once, hiding messages like 'Buy Popcorn' in movies to get people to buy more at the snack bar. It didn't work—and advertisers got in trouble for trying it. If any of the Grey films survived, you could study them by freezing the video or DVD frames to see if there was some message hidden in the film. But there's no copy anywhere."

"So they might have put a message like 'This is *really* scary' to make people think they were seeing something horrible," said Nancy.

"Uh-huh. But I doubt that happened way back then. More likely it's a case of old stories growing more fantastic the more people tell them."

"What would be really scary to you?" asked Nancy.

"I don't know. *Night of the Living Dead* zombies, I guess."

"Snakes would do it for me," said Nancy, with a shudder. "Alana," she called, loud enough to force her friend to remove her earphones. "What scares you the most?"

"Getting stuck on a perfectly good Saturday driving to a totally boring place with the two of you talking about totally boring old movies and junk."

"Spiders," said Alec. "Sis has arachnophobia."

"Wasn't that a movie?"

"Yeah—but it means fear of spiders. Spiders drive her crazy."

"Shut up," said Alana.

But he went on. "She even believes all those old stories about the girl who ratted her hair and never washed it and brushed against a tree so spiders got into her hairdo and ate into her brain."

"*Eeuuuww!*" cried Nancy.

"Shut up," Alana repeated. "I hate your talking about that stuff."

"There's another one about a woman who got bitten on the cheek by a spider, and the side of her face began to swell, and millions of baby spiders burst out when she went to the doctor."

Alana clamped her headphones back on and turned the volume up to the last notch.

A few moments later, they rounded a turn in the road. Alec pulled over and parked the car. "The old SSGG Studios," he announced.

"Where?" asked Nancy. Curious, Alana leaned between

the other two to look out the front window. "Oh, I see like part of a wooden wall over there—and there seems to be something behind that clump of trees. I guess that fire pretty well wiped everything out."

Alec got out a copy of an old photograph from the San Francisco Public Library. He stood beside the car, looking down at the photograph, then pointed out various things to Nancy. Alana remained sitting in the car, flipping through her CD folder.

"Those were the dressing rooms over there, and the editing rooms. There, where that bit of steel frame is still standing, was the main stage. The old carpentry and paint workshop would have been there, and the costumes there. The vaults where the film was stored would be right behind. That's where the fire began. I want to walk around, soak up the atmosphere. Are you coming?"

"Sure," Nancy responded.

"Alana?"

"I'm going to listen to music and soak up the sun."

"Enjoy yourself," said Alec. "Don't let the spiders bite."

He and Nancy set off exploring. Alana unrolled her bamboo beach mat, and peeled off her blouse and jeans to reveal the bathing suit underneath. Then she positioned the mat on dry grass, careful to avoid any logs or bushes or tumbled stones that might hide a dreaded spider. When she'd slathered on enough sunblock lotion and put on her Ray-Bans, she replaced her headphones and settled back to enjoy the day her way.

Something tickled her cheek. With a yelp, she brushed frantically, remembering Alec's spiders-in-the-face story. To her relief, it turned out to be only a leaf. She lay back down in the warmth, but now her mind was suddenly filled with spidery-grey images. She thought of a hairdo, veiled in grey cobwebs, alive with pale-grey spiders; she imagined a swollen cheek, the grey of dead skin swarming with unseen baby spiders. She also remembered the long, spidery fingers of the tall, willowy, ghostlike alien creature, called a "grey," that her mother had designed for the science fiction film Alana's parents were working on.

Eventually, she fell asleep, but she had nightmares of cobwebs and mist and tall beings whose skin rippled from swarms of tiny, living creatures teeming just below their dead, grey skin.

She awoke with a shudder, happy that the dream images were already fading from memory. But something was wrong. The sun had dropped to a late-afternoon position just above the horizon. She pulled up her dark glasses to look at her watch. It was almost 4 P.M. *Where were Alec and Nancy?* she wondered. *What could they have found that would hold their interest for nearly four hours?*

She pulled her jeans back on and buttoned her blouse. She started down the path through the brush and dry grass toward the spot where still-standing metal ribs marked the old main stage. It seemed as good a spot as any to begin her search. She called her brother's name, then her friend's, several times, but there was no answer. *Maybe they went on a hike farther up the canyon and lost track of time,* she thought.

In the lengthening shadows, the curved metal beams overhead—the glass panels they'd once supported having long since vanished—reminded Alana of a skeleton's rib cage.

To her disgust, the remains of the old building were thick with spider webs; in every corner and crevice, she could see the cottony grey shapes of egg sacs. She retreated quickly.

More calls got no response.

She followed the crumbling remains of a concrete path and suddenly found herself at the edge of what looked at first like an empty swimming pool, but which she quickly recognized as the foundation of a collapsed building. The bottom was littered with tumbled stone and twisted metal and fragments of wood—all showing traces of a fire. She remembered her brother talking about the vault where all the old movies had been stored—and where the fire that destroyed the studio had begun.

On the far side of the immense, blackened, sunken area, she found a path that led back into the thicker growth. Careful not to brush against any bushes that might hold spiders in ambush, she decided to follow the path a short way; she might meet Alec and Nancy coming back from the hike that seemed the only explanation for their long absence.

She had been following the zigzagging path for about twenty minutes when it suddenly ended in a sinkhole where the earth had fallen in to form a crater. To Alana, it looked as though the roof of a vast cave had suddenly dropped away. The edge of the crater was crumbly underfoot; if she wasn't careful, she realized, it could suddenly give way and she'd slide to the bottom, now heavily shadowed in the evening. *Could Alec and Nancy have fallen in?* she wondered anxiously.

She leaned over and called down, but there was no answer. Suddenly the seemingly solid ground she was leaning on gave way, and she started to slip down the wall.

Frantically, she scrambled back. She remembered sickening images from one natural history TV show of a bug called an "ant lion" that buried itself at the bottom of a funnel-shaped crater, a miniature version of the one she was struggling against. The insect hunter lurked, waiting for an unfortunate ant to tumble down the crumbling earth to become its dinner. Sudden fear gave her strength; she scraped her palms but managed to shove herself back to safety. There she sat breathing heavily. She shivered at the thought that her brother and her friend might have fallen in. She called again and again, but there was only silence. Telling herself that they might have gone in a thousand different directions—promising herself they were already back at the car waiting for her—she started to turn away from the pit.

There was movement at the bottom. Something rippled like grey cloth. She thought of spiders and their egg sacs, teeming with baby spiders about to be spewed into the world.

Careless now of the bushes and weeds that jabbed her hands and brushed her legs, she ran back down the hillside. At last, she broke free of them and reached the edge of the burned vault.

Alec and Nancy were sitting side by side on the edge of the sunken area, their legs dangling into the fire-charred opening.

"Hey, Sis, what's your hurry?" called Alec.

"You look like you've seen a ghost," added Nancy.

Seeing them, Alana suddenly felt like a fool for scaring herself. "I was worried about you," she said to hide her lingering fear.

"Here," Nancy invited, patting the edge of the foundation, "sit beside me. We've got a story to tell you."

Grey

"Shouldn't we get going?" said Alana. It was so late that the vault was filling with shadow, like ink in a swimming pool.

"Sit," Alec ordered.

When she sat, he continued, "We learned a lot about this place, and a lot about Grey. It would make a great science-fiction story, only it's true. The fire here . . ." He waved his hand over the deepening shadows below. ". . . wasn't an accident. It was set by August McGuire—the man himself. He was trying to get rid of Grey—oh, yes, Grey is quite real!—as well as the movies that he had made about the mysterious Grey. Seems McGuire learned that Grey was using the films to change audiences, mess with their minds. A little like that subliminal business we talked about earlier—but far more advanced."

"You're making this up," said Alana. "There's no way you could know any of this. And if you're trying to scare me, it isn't working." She started to get up, but Nancy grabbed her wrist and held on with surprising strength.

"Don't go yet," Nancy said.

"Grey comes from another place," Alec went on. "He came as planned, but something happened to the equipment that brought him here and was supposed to help him with his work."

"This is *so* boring," Alana said petulantly. "Space aliens conquer the world. Get real! Mom and Dad are *working* on this movie. Can't you come up with a better story than *that?*"

Alec ignored her. "Grey and what survived of the machinery wound up buried in these hills for years, until McGuire discovered them while building SSGG Studios.

155

They formed quite a team for years, until McGuire decided to save the world." Alec gave a harsh laugh that made Alana's skin crawl. "He almost succeeded, but a part of Grey escaped the fire, got to the still-buried machinery, and began healing. Grey has gotten stronger and has learned a few new tricks; he's discovered that the world has changed in ways that will help what Grey needs to do."

"Boo!" Alana sneered. "I'll catch the reruns on *Creature Features*." She jerked her arm free of Nancy's grasp.

"One last thing," said Alec. "Grey likes to play mind games; Grey enjoys scaring people." But Alana, angry at the others for their stupid attempt to frighten her, was already storming up the path.

She turned around. In the twilight, the two seated figures, with their backs to her now, suddenly looked pale as ghosts or mummies shrouded in pale rags and cobwebs. Even as she watched, they seemed to deflate, like balloons with slow leaks. Alana had the impression of greyness leaking out of them, puddling around the shrinking shapes. "Lights!" called Alec, from somewhere behind her.

"Cameras!" called Nancy.

"Action!" called a strange voice that sounded like dozens of voices blended together.

Alana was running now, through the dusky ruins of the old studio. But the skeleton of what had been was changing all around her into the studio of old. Walls sprang from foundations; the steel beams over the main stage healed themselves into perfect arches; glass panels grew to fill in the spaces. Alana spun frantically to avoid walls and doors and railings that hadn't been there a moment before. But everything was as colorless as the black-and-white photograph of the old studio that Alec had been looking at earlier.

"Alana," called the strange many-voices-in-one. Glancing over her shoulder, she saw a misty grey form gliding down the restored path that led between two workshops, their windows glowing with eerie grey light. Terrified beyond reason, she wrenched open the door before her, slammed it, and turned the lock, which gave a satisfyingly loud click. Only then did she look around her.

She was on the set of an old castle—as corny as the ones in the original *Dracula* movie her brother watched over and over. Above the black-and-white-painted stone walls, the first stars of evening glittered through the new glass panels. Lights flared soundlessly around her. Silence lay thick over everything. She opened her mouth to cry, "Help me, please, someone!" but no sound came out. It was as if her ears were plugged. *No,* she realized suddenly, *it's like I'm stuck in an old silent movie. Grey, whatever he is, is playing with my mind.*

She looked down and discovered that her blouse and jeans had changed into a gown like the women wore in *Dracula.* Out of the corner of her eye, she caught the movement of French doors blowing open, from a gust of wind generated by an unseen fan. Beyond the doors was the painted backdrop of English moors, with painted grey fog drifting over distant hills, while a painted grey-white moon was frozen in the night sky.

A shape appeared suddenly between the painted countryside and the balsa-wood French doors. The form was vague. The only thing Alana was certain of was its *greyness*—the grey of massed spiders' webs, of unhealthy flesh, of the painted mist cloaking the painted hills.

It moved closer. Now it looked more like a tall human figure draped in veils. Something like an arm drifted up; something like a finger beckoned her closer.

Against every instinct, she stepped nearer.

The veils billowed and churned. She knew what was going to happen. She had seen something like this in the old silent movie, *The Phantom of the Opera*—another favorite of her brother and parents—when the heroine discovers the Phantom and pulls his mask away to reveal the skull-like face underneath. This was the famous scene that had audiences fainting or turning away in horror.

The veils fluttered and seethed.

No more able to resist than *The Phantom*'s heroine, Alana raised her hand to the restless grey gauze.

For a moment, the rubbery grey face—exactly like one of her mother's latex sculptures of an alien grey—was both a shock and a relief.

Then the face *melted*. The hundreds of multilegged, multijointed creatures that were Grey dissolved in front of her, pooling around her feet.

Alana felt her mind—then all the rest of her—dissolving into the squirming, hungry, hypnotic greyness.

Which was just a preview of what happened to people everywhere when Grey accessed the Internet.

"Gulp!"

Now Tony knew what the feeling was whenever frightened live-action comedy or animated cartoon characters gave a big "Gulp!" He was standing on the porch of the immense, long-deserted Hampstead House, and his mouth and throat were suddenly filled with nervous saliva, so that he was ready to give the biggest "Gulp!" of all. But he didn't dare. He was sure that Patrick, Bernie, and Santos—his fellow "ghostbusters"—would laugh at any sign of fear. The others made a joke of the idea that the huge, rambling building was haunted. But they were curious enough to take an after-dark ramble through the place, just in case there might be something interesting to see. And they had been dared by a group of kids led by Leslie Wright.

Double-Dare to Be Scared

Tony, Patrick, and Santos were all wearing crucifixes. "Hey! It doesn't hurt to be safe, even if the stories about that place are bull-pucky," Patrick had said. So he had given Tony a silver cross that matched his own. "I took it out of my sister's jewelry box," Patrick had explained. "She never wears it." Santos wore a larger, gold cross around his throat, dangling above the "Island Pride" slogan on the T-shirt his brother had brought him back from Manila. Bernie had a Star of David, set with blue stones. "We're covered," he had said. "I saw this movie where crosses didn't work, because the vampire they dug up was Jewish." "What happens if the monster is Muslim or Buddhist?" Tony had asked—then laughed to show he was making a joke. From the looks his friends had given him, it wasn't a very good joke. "Sorry," he'd apologized. "Get serious," Patrick had advised.

So here they were on the half-collapsed porch of the Hampstead place. From the sidewalk, in the bright moonlight, the house almost gave the impression of a face. The double front doors—with their pattern of vertical raised stiles crossed with a single rail holding brass doorknobs—looked like skull's teeth clamped shut. A triangle of deep shadow above the doors suggested a nose. The matched clusters of second-story windows—boarded over—looked like blind eyes, which Tony imagined could watch in the uncanny way a skeleton's eyeless sockets could somehow see in a scary film.

Stop it! he ordered himself, *before the others see just how frightened you are.* He swallowed again, taking care to let no telltale "Gulp!" give him away as a coward and a baby.

Warning signs had been posted—"No Trespassing,"

"Gulp!"

"Trespassers will be prosecuted"—but no kids in the neighborhood paid attention. Some of the older guys had broken the lock one night and then wired the doors shut in a way that let anyone "in the know" waltz right in. Daring younger children would explore by daylight (daring only went so far when you were six or seven). At ten and eleven, Tony and his friends felt ready to chance the place by dark—provided that older kids, who sometimes used it as a gathering place, weren't around. They would run off anyone who invaded their turf. But tonight there were no teenagers around; most were attending the big play-off between the town's two high-school football teams. Patrick, the leader of the foursome, had chosen this evening with care.

Word was that some of the teens who partied in the darkened house had vanished, though newspaper reports dismissed the tales of strange disappearances as kids running away from home. In fact, most had been tracked down or had returned home on their own. Police had made one or two sweeps of Hampstead House but found nothing more than traces of illegal partying.

But the "underground news"—the "kids' news"—that was passed in excited whispers across the cafeteria tables or around the yard of Cameron Elementary School—assured eager listeners that the vanished ones had for sure been messing around Hampstead House. Rumors had sprung up about a crazy person hiding in a secret room, or a ghost or demon or monster, created or conjured up and left to prowl the place after a cult or coven or mad scientist had found the old building perfect for spooky doings. The stories were garbled, but they provided plenty of frightfully delightful fodder for the "kids' news."

In addition to the crosses and the Star of David, the boys had squirt guns filled with holy water. The idea had come from a movie Tony had seen; Santos had provided the holy water from Saint Agnes Church, which he and his family attended. Patrick also had a sterling-silver letter opener, which, he assured the others, was their backup, since silver scared off werewolves, vampires, and other nameless horrors.

And what horrors might, just might, be lurking inside the house? Tony wondered. This time he gulped so loud that Bernie heard him. But before Bernie could tease him about his nervousness, Patrick said quickly, "We'd better get going." Unwiring the front door, he added, "We've only got an hour and a half." The four were supposed to be at a Scout meeting; it was their cover to keep their parents from knowing what they were *really* up to. Hampstead House was officially "out of bounds" for all of them.

The doors swung wide. Blackness gaped and swallowed Patrick, who was in the lead. "Hurry up—and don't turn on your flashlights till we close the door." The other three entered: Santos eagerly, fingers folded around his crucifix; Bernie following cautiously, with nervous glances on either side; Tony coming last, able to step into the hungry blackness only out of fear of his friends' mockery.

"Close the door," ordered Patrick. Tony, nearest, shoved it closed. But the door started to swing back open because the lock was broken. *We're being given one last chance to get out,* thought Tony. *Run away now!*

"Gulp!"

"What's the matter with you?" hissed Patrick. He kicked the door shut, leaned against it until it stayed put, then snapped on his flashlight. "Find something heavy to keep it shut." The other boys added their flashlight beams to the search. Bernie spotted a mildewed throw rug. It was heavy and made a good doorstop. Once they were safe from outside discovery, they let their lights play more slowly over the hallway in which they stood.

Bernie and Santos inched closer to Tony on either side. Patrick was a few steps farther into the huge open space, but he suddenly seemed rooted in place, as though the desire to explore had left him.

They're just as scared as I am, Tony thought. *This is stupid! If there's nothing here, we're wasting our time. If there is something here, we could just disappear like those other kids.* But again, his fear of being the first one to admit his fear kept him silent. He clutched the silver cross with his left hand, while his right continued to swing his flashlight beam over the walls and ceiling and floor.

The boarded-up windows let in only slivers of moonlight. But the powerful flashlight beams (Patrick had insisted they all put in fresh batteries before entering the house) picked out the litter that lay strewn across the floorboards and the trash that was heaped in corners. Yellow newspapers, empty snack food packets, crushed soda and beer cans, cigarette butts—all were souvenirs of countless midnight parties over the years.

There were closed pocket doors to their left and right; ahead were two matching curved staircases that met high

overhead to become a single broad stairway climbing into the blackness of the upper story. The arrangement reminded Tony of a wishbone standing on its legs. Where the lower staircases joined, they formed an archway through which the boys could glimpse a hallway that ran back into the dark beyond reach of their flashlight beams. Under layers of dust and cobwebs, Tony could see shredded red draperies and the remains of red carpeting on the floor; it gave the impression of an open mouth, with a throat running back into the guts of the house. *What might be waiting at the end of that redness?* the boy wondered. *Something darker than the shadows? Something soft and squishy and slimy? Something with fangs and claws? Something hungry?* The more he tried to make himself stop thinking such nightmare thoughts, the harder his imagination worked. He was glad when Bernie, breaking the stillness, said, "I wonder what's in here." He pushed open the double doors on the left.

To their surprise, the heavy doors slid smoothly into the slots on either side as if they were freshly oiled. They all jumped back, half-expecting some monster to pop out at them as in a haunted house ride. But there was just more darkness inside. The others clustered in the doorway to check out the room; to Patrick's disappointment (and to Tony's relief), they found just a dining room table, tilting crazily because one of its legs was broken off, and a bunch of beaten-up dining room chairs lying on their sides or backs.

"Let's go," said Patrick. Tony and Santos followed him out into the hall, but Bernie said suddenly, "Hey! What's that?" and ducked back into the room. The doors suddenly slid from their grooves and slammed together. There was a click as if a lock had caught. They could hear Bernie inside, tugging and pushing at the doors, but the heavy, dark wood panels remained firmly sealed.

"You jerk!" yelled Patrick, as he and Tony and Santos tried to pry the doors open. "What did you do?"

"Nothing!" came Bernie's voice, muffled by the heavy door. "Get me out of here."

"It's really stuck!" said Tony, who had dug his fingertips into the groove where the doors met.

Inside Bernie was alternately beating on the door and slapping at the wood in frustration.

"Bern!" Patrick shouted, his mouth close to the door. "There's got to be another door there—just find the back way out! Man! I have to tell you guys everything!" he added in disgust.

"There's another door way at the back of the room. But it's closed, too."

"That doesn't mean it's locked. Go try it."

"I'm opening it." Bernie's voice was faint but clear. "There's a hallway with shelves. It's really dark in there."

"Just find your way out. We'll go down the hall under the steps. We'll all meet in the kitchen or someplace back there."

"I don't think I can. It's too creepy," Bernie whined.

"Fine, then stay there. We'll send the fire department to chop you out. I'm sure your folks will be happy about that."

"I'm going," Bernie said, now sounding more sulky than frightened.

A minute later they heard a door slam. At the same moment, the pocket doors rolled aside. A faint sound like a gentle sigh came from the room beyond.

"Gulp!"

"You guys lean against those doors so they don't close," Patrick ordered. "I'll go get Bernie. The Big Baby."

Tony and Santos stationed themselves on either side, making sure the doors didn't slip shut. They watched Patrick rattle the knob, then kick the back door, but he couldn't get the panel to budge.

"What is it with that guy? That's the second door he's screwed up."

"Maybe it's the house," said Tony.

"Maybe there was something waiting in the dark to grab him," said Santos, fishing his holy-water filled squirt-gun out of his pocket.

"Maybe you guys are nuts," said Patrick, but Tony thought, *He's talking like he isn't scared. But I can see it in his eyes.*

"He's somewhere in the house. We'll find him," Patrick insisted. "C'mon." He headed for the hall shouting Bernie's name. Santos called, too. But Tony found he didn't want to shout or call attention to himself. With the others making so much racket, he could allow himself a couple of good gulps. He could feel his nervousness growing with every step they took deeper into the dark house.

The hall carpet and hangings stank of mildew and rot. Tony frequently had to brush aside spider webs, as he followed the others deeper inside. But all their shouts of "Bernie!" brought no answering call. There were several shut doors on either side of the passage; they opened them all as they passed but found nothing of interest—and no trace of Bernie.

At the end of the hall was a heavy door, with rows of thick frosted-glass panes set in wood frames. It was sealed fast. Patrick leaned close, rubbed the dust off one glass square, and tried to look through it. Then he held his flashlight against the glass, but it didn't help. He called Bernie's name a couple more times, then listened with his ear against the glass. "I think I hear something. C'mere, Santos—you listen, too." The other boy obediently put his ear to a nearby pane. "Let's shout together," suggested Patrick. The two shouted, "Bernie!" then paused to listen, then shouted again. "Now I think maybe I heard something," said Santos.

While they experimented, Tony, who thought he'd heard something, too, took a few hesitant steps back down the red hall, holding his flashlight out in front of him like a lightsaber. "Bernie, that you?" he whispered, not daring to make a louder sound. To his surprise, the doors they had left open as they explored the hall were now shut. Suddenly they began to pop open, one by one, starting at the far end of the corridor. Each one flung open with a wet, sucking sound that reminded him of the sound a trout had made when he had gone fishing with his father the first time. He still recalled feeling faintly sick as the creature writhed and gasped on the pier. But these sounds were a gazillion times louder.

The noise made his friends turn suddenly. They gaped in terror at the display. Tony himself was frozen in place. He felt his throat working, trying to swallow, trying to suck in air, but he was choking on his fear. Santos began to run; Patrick, too. But Patrick was too slow. The glass door behind him suddenly burst open; a dark bundle of something wrapped around his waist. In a flicker he was pulled into the darkness as the door banged shut. Santos shot past Tony, pushing the other boy out of the way as he fled down the hall, the light from his flashlight bobbing crazily.

There was a *pop,* a *whish,* and Santos grunted like someone punched in the stomach. Then Santos and his light were gone, swallowed as suddenly as if a knife had cut him off from the world. Far down the hallway, a door slammed. A moment later the faintest breeze drifted past Tony's ear, as his legs remained locked in terror. Again, he half-heard the sound like a soft little satisfied sigh.

I'm alone in the house with whatever's behind those doors, thought Tony. Desperately, he swung his flashlight up and down the hallway. Behind him, the light splashed off the dusty glass panes on the fatal door. Ahead, as far down the hallway as his beam reached, he saw only closed doors and the distant, slightly less dark hallway entrance. *Maybe, just maybe, whatever's hiding here will have enough with the others. Maybe it—they—whatever—will let me go.* He knew he was being horrible, thinking only of himself, hoping the others could somehow buy his escape from Hampstead House.

Hurry up, he told himself. *Don't wait for what's in the dark to come and get you.*

Amazingly, though he was trembling all over, though his legs felt unsteady as rubber bands and his mouth and throat were so dry that only a tiny sound like mud cracking—no "gulp"—could emerge, he managed to get moving. He advanced down the hall, swinging the flashlight back and forth the way he'd seen heroes wave a torch to drive off beasts in a jungle or zombies on a rampage.

With each step, he felt a bit surer. He dreaded passing each door, for fear it would fling open, and something—hands, tentacles, claws—would grab at him. But the hall remained calm; the doors stayed shut. He passed under the ragged drapes at the passage's end and into the hallway beyond. Across from him, the flashlight beam picked out the old rug still holding the front door closed.

Safe, he thought, *safe, safe, safe.*

He was just dragging the rug back from the door when, behind him, the hallway was suddenly filled with the wet, popping sound of every door being flung open. Turning with a groan, his last thought was: *It's not anything in the house. It's the house itself.*

From the hallway shot a thick mass of red—the rotting carpet suddenly turned into a lengthy tongue, like an iguana's. It wrapped around Tony's waist and yanked him into the blackness. The flashlight flew from his hand, crashed against a wall, and went out.

A single vast *"GULP!"* echoed through the rooms where all the doors stood open.

Then every door slammed shut, and a contented silence settled over the moonlit house.